I0517226

British soap star Marius Treadway's week has gone to hell. Still reeling from a failed romance, he quit his TV show only to learn that his sizable business investments are nothing but scams. Depressed and needing time to rethink his future, he travels to the island of Capri to visit his long-lost Uncle Toppy and twin cousins, Zeca and Alex.

At first, life seems relaxing and enjoyable on the sun-drenched, lemon-scented island, but it soon becomes clear that Alex's private hotel is being targeted for crime, possibly because it's gay-owned. Then, one of the oldest gay business owners in Capri Town finds his store trashed.

Determined to help his family, Marius soon meets dazzling Brazilian soccer player Crisanto Alvarez, who makes a play for him. Can it really be that, underneath it all, the Isle of Capri is a healer of hearts?

CONTENT ADVISORY: This is a re-release title. It was originally released under the title ISLE OF CAPRI.

Relentless Obsession
Copyright © 2019 A.J. Llewellyn
ISBN: 978-1-4874-2498-5
Cover art by Martine Jardin

Published by eXtasy Books Inc or
Devine Destinies, an imprint of eXtasy Books Inc

Look for us online at:
www.eXtasybooks.com or www.devinedestinies.com

Relentless Obsession
Relentless Book 3

By

A.J. Llewellyn

DEDICATION

In memory of actor Leslie Grantham, the best baddie in soap operas.

Trademarks Acknowledgement

The author acknowledges the trademarked status and trademark owners of the following wordmarks mentioned in this work of fiction:

Alitalia: Alitalia-Compagnia Aerea Italiana SpA Corporation Italy
BAFTA: British Academy of Film and Television Arts
BBC: The British Broadcasting Corporation
Canfora: A. Canfora SNC
Chanel: Chanel, Inc.
Cristal: Champagne Louis Roederer S.A.
Diner Dash: GLU Mobile Inc.
Dolce Far Niente: music and lyrics by Meredith Willson
Ettinger: G. Ettinger Ltd
Fawlty Towers: BBC / BBC Worldwide
Ferrari: Ferrari S.p.A. Joint Stock Company Italy
Galliano: John Galliano S.A. Joint Stock Company France
Giacomo Conterno: Azienda Vitivinicola Conterno Giacomo di Conterno Giovanni Società Agricola S.S. Entreprise
Google: Google Inc.
iPad: Apple Inc.
Joe Snyder: Joe Snyder S.A. de C.V.
LA Galaxy: Major League Soccer
LEGO: Lego Juris A/S Corporation
Lojack: Lojack Corporation
Miranda: BBC Two & BBC One
Realtor: National Association of Realtors Corporation

Ristorante Le Grottelle: Via Arco Naturale, Capri NA, Italy

Sciuscia and Sciorbi: Via XX Settembre, Camogli, Genova, Italy

Skype: Microsoft Corporation / Skype Technologies SA Corporation

Taser: TASER International, Inc.

The Godfather: Paramount Pictures

The Thick of It: BBC Four & BBC Two/BBC HD

Trattoria Pizzeria Al Buco: Viale Tommaso De Tommaso, Anacapri NA, Italy

UNESCO: United Nations Educational Scientific Cultural Organization

Yelp: Yelp Inc.

YouTube: Google Inc.

Zeffirino: Via XX Settembre, Genova, Italy

CHAPTER ONE

"Hi, Uncle Toppy." I'd rehearsed these three words maybe a dozen times since I'd hopped on a plane the day before from Athens to Capodichino Airport in Naples. For somebody who'd spent the last twelve years plying his trade as a professional actor, my words fell flat. I didn't sound relaxed and confident. I sounded stressed and frightened.

Which I was.

I'd spent the night in a small, very noisy hotel in the city center, wondering if I should just show up on the island of Capri and hope for the best. Would my uncle be receptive to my visit? I'd called his restaurant several times, but the phone just rang and rang.

I had debated this during a long, sleepless night. I'd called his house phone number first thing this morning, and some woman answered, screaming at me that I was disturbing her bread. At least, that's what I understood of her rapid-fire Italian.

Obviously, I was wrong. How can you disturb bread?

And now, here I was, my uncle standing behind the bar of Café Toppy, which, according to Yelp was one hell of a hit on Capri. I'd traveled from Naples by the first-morning ferry. A strange little train thingy at the base of a cliff had trundled me up the mountain. I'd walked up to what I now knew was the main street of Capri Town. I'd asked a few people if they knew where Café Toppy was and got encouraging smiles and lots of finger pointing.

I also got more exercise than I'd had in months. I sup-

1

posed I shouldn't have felt disappointed that nobody came to greet me at the train stop, but I did. Damn it, I did.

"Uncle Toppy!" I shouted. It took him another moment to hear me over the frantic whine of the cappuccino machine and Italian opera playing over the sound system.

I hadn't seen him in three years, but I'd worked hard to keep my connection going with him.

He stared at me now over the tops of his eyeglasses. I didn't expect to see him like this. I'd imagined he'd be sitting by a pool sunning himself, watching the world sail by on an azure sea, some beautiful signorina bringing him mimosas.

Instead, he looked as stressed as I felt. He had a coffee at his elbow and a screwdriver in his hand. He squinted at me.

"Holy crud with salt and pepper on a bagel. What the hell are you doing here, Marius?"

"You didn't get my messages?"

He shook his head. As family reunions went, this one wasn't going so well. He seemed more interested in tangling with his coffee machine than talking to me. He began poking at the machine again.

"I left them on your cell phone. I also called your house this morning."

"Oh." He stopped. "You're the one who disturbed Angie's baking."

"So she was talking about bread." I chuckled. "And I thought my Italian was way off."

"Mate, she goes barmy if I even whisper in her ear when she's baking. How'd you get her number anyway?"

"You sent it to me."

"I did? I must have been drunk."

Well! I didn't know what to say to that, and then he asked in a conspiratorial way, "What do you know about fixing cappuccino machines?"

"I don't. I'd Google for help."

2

He pulled a face. "All right, Marius. What did you say you're doing here?"

"I've got no place else to go."

"That's comforting. What happened?"

"I OD'd. That was after I had brain surgery, got gang-raped in the emergency room, got put on life support, received a heart transplant and then found out I was the father of mutant triplets."

He stared at me, wide-eyed now. "You had mutant triplets? Shit." He tossed the screwdriver into the sink. "That damned soap opera gets worse storylines instead of better."

"Tell me about it."

"But I heard you won a BAFTA."

"Not me, Uncle Toppy. I just got nominated." I tried not to sound embittered when I added, "For the twelfth straight year in a row."

"I never got nominated once, and I'm a bloody legend," he said, without a trace of sarcasm in his tone. "You've got money up the wazoo, and you've still got your looks, and you were killed off a big show in a spectacular way, so what brings you here?"

"No . . . my departure was open-ended. They are hoping I change my mind."

He frowned. "I thought you said they killed you off?"

"No. I said I OD'd. My last scene I shoot up and run off and fall in a river. The Thames. In the middle of frickin' winter. No idea how I survived, but I did it in one take."

He looked impressed. "Nice way to go. That opens up all sorts of possibilities if you ever decide to go back."

"Oh, no. Never." I took a deep breath. "That's partly why I don't want to go back to London. I've spent my entire working life on that show. Everything's fallen apart, Uncle Toppy, and I'm afraid if I return to England I'll go back and have more triplets. Or maybe . . . I'll become a mutant

3

myself."

He shook his head. "No, no. We can't have that."

Easy for him to say. I'd been a hostage to that soap opera and my character, Rufus Dickinshaw, for twelve years. It was time to move on.

"So what are you doing here?" he asked again, shoving his glasses back up his nose.

"Well, I bought an apartment building just outside of Athens three years ago . . . before all the troubles started there. I've sunk everything into it. I got ripped off by an attorney and a Greek realtor, and I've paid the damned Greek government a fortune, and I've lost . . . a lot." I swallowed hard. I still couldn't believe it. A cup of coffee sure would have been nice right now.

"You want a coffee?" he asked as if reading my mind.

"Isn't the machine broken?"

"Of course it's not bloody broken. I always pretend it is first thing in the morning because I still don't know how to use it. It stops people from ordering coffee until Zeca gets in." He eyed the wall-clock. "Which should be anytime now."

I stared up at the clock. It was shaped like a lemon. The lemon motif, in fact, seemed to dominate the café.

"How is Zeca?" I asked.

"Fabulous. Both the boys are doing great. Capri's done them wonders." He reached under the counter and held up a coffee pot. "This is my secret stash I brew on the stove. Want a cup?"

"Sure. Thanks." I watched him pour me a cup. A touristy looking couple walked in, and Toppy immediately got busy with the screwdriver again. The couple looked at me. She recognized me, I could tell that right away. She snapped my photo with her cell phone. *Fuck a duck.* I'd hoped to get away from stuff like that.

There was a clatter of activity, and I felt, rather than heard, a burst of testosterone, and there was my cousin Zeca, accompanied by a tall, handsome Italian-looking guy who took my breath away. He oozed sexuality in his jeans and white silk shirt, the sleeves rolled up to his elbows. Zeca grinned at me and came over and hugged me.

He looked amazing. Tan, his dark hair cut short, his eyes sparkled with happiness. There is a strong family resemblance between me and my twin cousins Zeca and Alex, except for the sparkling happiness part.

Zeca introduced me to his companion, Antonio, who shook my hand. If I was in any doubt as to the nature of their relationship, Antonio put that to rest kissing by Zeca passionately right on the lips.

"Call me bello," he told Zeca. "Nice meeting you," he said over his shoulder to me and left.

Wow. Nice ass.

"You want a cappuccino?" Zeca asked me, "Or do you prefer Toppy's mud?"

"Erm—" I hadn't had a chance to try the mud . . . I mean, coffee, yet, but I knew Toppy was a proud man. "This is perfect," I said. I took a sip and almost keeled over. I could have stripped paint with his concoction.

"What's with the face?" Toppy's expression turned dark. He became distracted by the tourists who wanted their picture taken with him. Ah, now this was the Toppy I knew. A total camera whore. He flipped the screwdriver over his shoulder and rushed to the other side of the counter.

"I'll make you a cappuccino." Zeca began working the machine, which purred under his expert touch. "Here, I'll tip this out," he said under his breath. "He'll think you drank it." My cousin smiled at me. "Long time no see."

"Yeah."

"How's life on the soap?"

"I made them kill me off."

5

"I thought you said it was open-ended," Toppy said, returning to the counter.

"It is. But in my mind, I'm killed off."

"So, it's a good thing, right?" Zeca's lovely brown eyes looked concerned. He was the warmer of the twins. Alex was the good-time guy. He always made me think of Charlie Sheen with less booze, no broads, and better dress sense.

Zeca's cell phone rang, and he turned all gooey. "It's my man." He texted with one hand, frothing milk with the other.

"The one who just left?" I was stunned.

"They're goofy," Toppy said, his smile indulgent.

I caught a glimpse of Zeca's wedding ring. "Are you married?"

"Not yet." He laughed. "Alex is getting married in the fall, though."

"Alex?" I couldn't believe my ears. "He can't sit still long enough to have a cup of coffee, let alone get married."

"He's a different man." Zeca beamed at me. "He and his partner, Hugh, have a small, very discreet, private hotel on Belvedere of Tragara, a very ritzy street here. They cater to gay travelers. They're booked for the next six months, even during the offseason."

Zeca looked so proud, and I was happy for Alex, really I was. But it seemed to me that my cousins and my uncle were all kinda . . . livin' large on this small island, and I'd lost all hope. In Athens yesterday afternoon when I realized I couldn't gamble what little money I had left, I could have gone to Berlin, like almost thirty thousand Greeks have done over the last twelve months.

But no. Something in me . . . some deep inner voice had told me to head to Capri.

"Come into the kitchen and talk to me." Toppy clapped my shoulder, then picked up my suitcase and laptop bag.

"They want the pizza omelets and toast," he told Zeca, "and of course your famous cappuccinos."

Zeca slid me two cups of coffee, and we were on our way.

I'd had pleasant visions of sitting by a sunlit window eating warm bread and dunking it in coffee. But no. Like all my other dreams lately, big and small, this one was left wanting.

Toppy stashed my bags against the kitchen wall. The room was huge, and I noticed a wood-fire stove and tons of pots. Everything looked clean.

He fiddled with a speaker on a rustic wooden shelf. "I gotta get Antonio to fix this thing. I can't cook without music. What do you know about fixing these things?"

"Nothing, Uncle."

He flashed me a look that told me I was useless. Now I was beginning to worry. I had no discernible food skills, apart from the fact that I like to eat it.

Uncle Toppy gave up on the speaker and came over to me. "Here. Chop some onions and pepperoni." He handed me two plastic containers from the fridge and a big, fancy chopping knife. At least I assumed it was. It looked like a half moon and had two wooden knobs on either side of it.

"What's this?"

"A double mezzaluna, dummy. Hmmm . . . you're half Italian, and you didn't know that?"

"I'm not Italian. I'm half Greek and half English, remember?"

"Oh . . . yeah." He gave me a sympathetic pat on the shoulder. "It's the English part of you. No cooking skills to speak of."

I would have argued about that, except he kept talking. The British have a reputation for being lousy cooks, but Chef Gordon Ramsay and so many others had changed all that. Hadn't they?

"Here's how it works." Toppy took a bunch of thinly

sliced pepperoni out of the container, plopped it on the wooden chopping block and began rocking the double mezzaluna across the cured meat and back again. Then he turned the strips around and did it once more. He got small, uniform pieces.

"Chop the onions," he said. "Please."

I thought I could do that. I began peeling one and sliced into it. He sighed when he saw me crying.

"Is that the onions making you boo-hoo or life?"

"A bit of both," I admitted.

"There, there. You're home now." He patted my head the way he used to do when I was a kid, and I'd just let Alex talk me into eating dirt or something.

"Marius, can you shred cheese, or will that give you a complete breakdown?"

I blinked through tears I didn't really want to shed. "No, I can manage."

"How brave." He handed me another container. "Wash your bloody hands first! We don't want onions on everything."

Boy, he was a tyrant in the kitchen. Back on *The Fletchers*, the soap opera we'd been on together, he'd been a darling. Supportive, wonderful, funny . . . and now I came to think of it, an absolute bastard when he'd had a night on the beer.

I washed my hands, comforted by the smell of sizzling butter and onions. The back door blew open and a woman charged in brandishing a basketful of fresh breadsticks. She looked like a young Sophia Loren, if Sophia Loren were spitting mad and trying to kick somebody with her pointy-toed shoes.

"Sii gentile," Toppy hissed at her as he took the bread from her. I understood he was telling her to be nice.

"My bread is bad." She narrowed her eyes and pointed a long red talon at me. "Because of you, no?" Her English was

8

broken and heavy . . . but I got the point.

Maybe coming to Capri wasn't the best idea I'd had after all.

I didn't respond. I wasn't sure if I could handle lady violence so early in the day.

"The cheese ain't gonna shred itself, mutant maker. Get busy." Toppy handed me a big black tin with a silver grated side on top. I picked up the wheel of cheese that had a pretty label reading Friulano. It smelled like cheddar. I got busy as he'd suggested, nay demanded. This was the most cooking I'd done in my entire adult life and, at the age of thirty, I hadn't planned on doing this much.

Zeca suddenly stormed in. I'd just realized Toppy was busy mauling Sophia Loren against the door. Zeca's gaze swept the kitchen and, with a stoic air, he prepared two omelets faster than I could have finished chopping a single carrot.

"Toast," he barked at Toppy, who gave him a weird look. No. Not weird. Petrified.

"Toast?" Sophia Loren echoed. She seemed very upset we were about to mutilate her bread and went mad with a stream of Italian. "*Succiacazzi!*" she screamed, pointing at me. She'd just called me a cocksucker.

Only in my dreams, I thought.

Toppy tried covering her mouth with his, and she kneed him in the balls. He fell on his back like a cockroach, doubled up in pain. She took off, and Toppy eventually got to his knees, his face a scary shade of purple.

"Welcome to Capri," he croaked, crawling off to the bathroom just as the toaster popped and Zeca caught two slices of thick white bread and buttered them.

"Need help?" I asked.

He shook his head and glanced at the closed bathroom door. "There's a bag of frozen peas in the freezer. Can you

9

get them for Dad?" He looked pained. "Dad and Angie had a bad breakup. He was dating someone else for a while, but they just got back together. I think he must love drama. All they do is fuck and fight."

"Love sucks," I said.

Zeca gazed at me. "What happened to that cute Italian actor you were dating? The one who did all those horror movies?"

"Paulo went to Hollywood. He changed his cell phone number. Haven't heard from him since."

I got the frozen peas and took them to Toppy, who limped out of the bathroom. He sat in the only chair in the kitchen. I noticed it was Toppy's director's chair from *The Fletchers*.

"Zeca, baby, make Daddy a little coffee, will you?" he whined, pressing the peas to his crotch.

Yep. Love left its mark, physical, mental or both. It also sent warning signals most of us cheerily ignore. That was the first thing that had gone wrong. I should have seen the signs. Paulo had persuaded me to give up my show. We'd move to Greece. We'd talked of getting married in Madrid. How foolish it all seemed now.

"Some men are bastards," Zeca said and left the kitchen.

Over the next couple of hours, I tried to make myself useful and adjusted to Uncle Toppy bossing me around. I found I was most helpful to him and Zeca by collecting glasses, spoons, and dishes. I discovered that my cousin had an unhealthy phobia about running out of spoons. He seemed obsessed to me.

Toppy showed me the way they liked to wash the glasses, cups, and spoons by hand. He made me wear only one glove because he said I needed one hand free to rinse and dry. They couldn't wait long enough for the dishwashers to go through a load. The plates and cooking pots and all the utensils went through a heavy wash cycle in detergent that smelled like lemons. That was nice. Other than that, frankly, I found the morning traumatizing.

"It's my own brand," Toppy told me when I mentioned the lemon soap. "I sell it in the café."

I'd done two loads when he finally gave me some time to talk to him right after the morning rush.

"We have a fifteen-minute window," he said. "Then bedlam strikes again. What are your plans, kid?" We walked outside the café and parked ourselves at one of the suddenly empty tables.

"I don't know, Uncle Toppy." I was exhausted. Not from my work in the kitchen but my life in general. I'd thought I'd been so careful, saving my money, investing it . . . I still had my apartment in West Kensington, in London, and I'd rented it out. That would bring me some income. Waking up and not rushing to the studio set in Ealing was a reality that was just starting to hit me.

For the first time in twelve years, I had no schedule, and I was floundering. The difficulty was in trying to decide what to do with the rest of my life. I'd had plans to live and write in Greece, but my apartment building had been totally destroyed in the riots last year, and I'd had no idea.

"I've been working sixteen-hour days, and I was led along by a disreputable real estate agent who told me the building had sustained some damage," I said. "We stayed in touch by text and cell phone calls. We even Skyped, and she was charming. I believed her. She kept billing me for repairs of all kinds and told me tenants had fled. I believed that, too. I'd stayed abreast of the horrible problems in Greece, particularly Athens."

Uncle Toppy was staring at me. He let me ramble.

"I kept sending her money, but when my bank in Athens

11

contacted me asking when I was going to follow the government's instructions and demolish what was left of the building, I flew straight to the city to check on things."

"When was this?"

"Two weeks ago, two days after I'd finished my last episode of the series."

It had hit me harder than I thought. I expected to maybe get rid of some stuff, take my time moving to Greece. I'd left one apartment empty for me to move into.

My parents, who lived in London, had persuaded me to rent my flat fully furnished through a company that rents to tourists looking for an 'at home' experience. My mother had handled everything with surprising ease. And now . . . I was without a home. I'd promised my London digs to the rental company for the next two years.

Telling Toppy all of this was devastating.

"So this realtor was scamming you the whole time?"

I nodded. "Her husband's an attorney. I met them through my dad."

"He's a plonker," Toppy said. He had every right to think so. We'd had a rough history we had to agree to overlook the day we started working together on the soap. I was the son of Toppy's ex-wife's brother. The ex-wife I knew had once kidnapped Alex and Zeca and almost got them killed in a train wreck. It had ruined our wonderfully tight, close-knit family existence.

My parents still acted weird about Toppy. After the kidnapping, they had never wanted family dinners . . . or holiday celebrations. But for me, there was something about Toppy and the twins I couldn't let go of. I became an actor because Toppy was one. He'd mentored me. He'd been good to me. But ultimately, he had always wanted to be a restaurateur and here he was.

He'd quit the show a few years ago and never looked

back. I realized now that he hadn't been lying to me whenever we talked on the phone. I could see the café was damned hard work, but as I watched him and Zeca flitting around all morning, I could tell it was their passion. They loved what they were doing.

"I don't think you made a mistake investing your money, and it's possible you can get compensation from the Greek government . . . eventually," he said. "It'll be years before they sort out the mess. In the meantime, I can help you get a good European Economic Community attorney. Those guys are cleaning up all the scams, but I don't want it to define your existence, okay?"

"Okay." Suddenly I felt better. Toppy had a way of just saying things, making it all seem sensible, reasonable.

"You did good, kid. You invested your money like we talked about. But for future reference, invest where you can keep your eye on the prize."

Yeah, he was right about that.

He called out to Zeca for two more coffees.

"You seem so happy working," I said. I still couldn't get over that. I thought he was over here living the good life.

"Work is love made visible." Toppy grinned just as Alex crossed the terrazza over to us. He looked great, too. He seemed so pleased to see me, and within minutes, Zeca was with us, the four of us 'gas bagging,' as my mother would have called it, over coffee. They heard my whole sorry saga, since Toppy made me repeat it all.

"You can stay at the house with me." Toppy had a thoughtful look on his face. "You can sit around like a dilettante and write, or . . ." His voice drifted off.

"Or?" I asked.

He kept stirring his coffee. "Zeca's room is free. He's moved in with Antonio. Hugh and Alex have a room. They sometimes use it to get away from their pesky patrons."

"They're not pesky," Hugh said.

"Yes, they are," Toppy said. "Let's just call a spade a shovel here. I read some of their Yelp comments. Those little cretins."

Alex, Zeca, and I laughed.

"Now, Marius, I believe in the value of hard work," Toppy said. "You'll learn more about life working here than you ever did on that stupid TV show."

I opened my mouth to protest, but he said, "No, no, don't thank me. Now listen. I don't need rent from you, but I could really use your help here. You're a natural, kid."

Yeah, a natural klutz. Didn't he see me stumble around here like Blind Freddie?

"You can wait tables. You'll get paid, of course. You'll get great tips. You will meet a guy. A great guy. Both my Zeca and my Alex met their husbands right here working at this café."

"Really?"

The twins nodded.

Toppy went on. "Oh, and you can have your pick of lunch or evening shift."

I wanted to say that I wasn't a waiter. I liked being waited on, but I saw the hope in my cousins' eyes.

"Erm . . ."

When I caught both twins mouthing the word lunch at me, I said, "I'll take lunch."

"Good." Toppy seemed so happy. "That gives you the rest of the time to write and figure out if that's what you want."

Toppy's lady-friend walked by us. I saw the way she looked at him. I wasn't sure if it was desire or a passion to kill. He leered at her. I saw the worried looks the twins exchanged.

But Toppy, oblivious, extended his hand to me. "We got

ourselves a deal?"

"Yes."

We all shook hands.

"Welcome home," Alex said. I knew he meant it.

As I picked up my cup to enjoy the last, delicious sip of coffee left in it, I spotted a tall, dark and sexy man jogging toward us. My God, he was gorgeous. Dressed head to toe in black, his hooded sweatshirt slipped back, and I glimpsed his golden features. He was so hot I missed my mouth with the coffee cup and liquid ran down my chin.

For one brief second, our gazes held, and I could swear he smiled at me, but it was a kind smile. And then he passed us by.

And suddenly I felt I had been right to come here. A door had closed on my dreams, but a window, just a little one, had opened in my mind, and a small breeze carrying the scent of lemons wafted over me . . .

Chapter Two

I was drained, utterly wiped out, by the time Toppy took me up the nine million stone stairs to his picturesque terrace house built into the mountainside. He wanted me to have an early siesta, then work the lunch shift. I wanted to sleep forever, but I'd seen how shorthanded they were. He told me they'd had a lot of staff turnover lately.

"We have lunch late here on the island. And dinner, too. I'll make sure somebody wakes you in time."

He gave me a huge iron key, the type they use in computer time management games as secret clues. Computer . . . I hadn't checked for emails or news in a few days now. Finding Internet cafés that were up and running had been difficult in Athens. It had been a shock, arriving there to see my beautiful apartment building looking like a bombed-out shell. Most of the city had been like a ghost town.

I'd stayed in a bed and breakfast on the outskirts of the city because most of the businesses in Athens were closed. Chain metal covered even the main pharmacies. The government wouldn't give store owners permission to open.

It all seemed arbitrary and confusing, not to mention unfair. Those stores that were open had huge sales going on. What haunted me, as Toppy showed me my room, was that I was here in a lovely house . . . and Greece was still in shambles.

"I'm gonna be next door at Angie's but do not to call me unless the house is on fire, okay?"

Too tired to respond, I lay on Zeca's bed fully clothed and

fell asleep immediately. My tortured mind treated me to an unpleasant kaleidoscope of images of all the homeless animals I'd seen in Athens. People had just dumped their dogs and cats. I tossed and turned, awakened finally by Zeca who gazed down at me.

"You okay, Marius?"

I slowly opened my eyes, realizing I was in tears.

"Alex thinks you should take it easy the rest of the day." He handed me some tissues. "You've had a really bad time, huh?"

I sat up. "Yeah." My eyes felt puffy and my emotions raw.

"Have you been online at all?" he asked.

I shook my head.

"Somebody took a photo of you in the restaurant today and put it on the Internet. People know you're here now. The photo caption says you are waiting on tables." He took a deep breath. "I'm sorry, cuz."

I shrugged. "Don't be."

"No. That's not how we do things here. Listen, Antonio's here. He's downstairs. Why don't you take a quick shower and come down and talk to him? He wants to help."

"How can he help?"

"He's the local cop."

"Oh." I'd had no idea. Zeca showed me the linen press where once again everything smelled like lemons. His suggestion of a shower was perfect. I felt so much better after it. I returned to the bedroom, opened up my suitcase and pulled out fresh jeans and a white T-shirt. The room was very nice now that I was awake enough to take it all in. Dominated by a double bed pushed against the wall, a dresser, chair, and closet, it had a charming, rustic feel. All of it had been capped off by what looked like a computer cart sporting a bunch of yellow daisies in a vase.

I dressed quickly and went downstairs. Zeca and Antonio

were on the sofa, all over each other. Zeca kissed his lover, gave me a wink and left the house. Antonio didn't look so thrilled as he watched his man walk out the door, but he smiled at me and extended a hand to the chair opposite him.

"Please, Marius, take a seat." He leaned forward and held my gaze. "First, I want to apologize for the invasion of your privacy. Capri is the one place we want celebrities to feel comfortable."

I fidgeted in my seat. "But I don't . . . I'm not a celebrity."

He smiled at me. "Well, this . . . photographer," he spat the word out. "Seems to think so. I found out who he is, and I told him he's not welcome to walk into our restaurant and take pictures of family members and post them on the Internet."

"That was nice of you, thank you."

"It won't be happening again. We forbid this type of bullshit here. We are not Hollywood, where the waiters and waitresses earn money tipping off the paparazzi when a celebrity walks into their restaurant. And you're family. Two reasons for me to get tough with this character." His gaze grew intense. "You're related to . . . her, aren't you?"

I knew he was talking about my aunt, the twins' mother.

"Yes, but we're not close."

He nodded. "So, she's not planning on coming here?"

I understood his concern then. Zeca had spent months in the hospital with a broken back after sustaining massive injuries in the train crash. His mother had barely visited him. She'd gone off to Majorca with her lover.

"No. She's not. She has no idea I'm here . . . unless she's seen today's photo. To be honest, I haven't even told my parents yet. As for my aunt, I haven't seen her in years. She borrowed money from my parents and never paid it back, so relations are strained. Besides which, she doesn't approve of gays."

That seemed to surprise him.

I went on. "I heard from my father that she has a new lover and they own a pub in Somerset. She moonlights as a tarot reader . . . but I wouldn't give her sixpence for one of her psychic predictions."

Actually, I'd paid her more, but he didn't need to know that. The last time I'd seen her was three years ago at a Greek Easter dinner my parents had. She'd insisted on telling my fortune, and I'd driven to her home in the country where, over a two-hour session, she'd urged me to buy the apartment building in Athens. She'd also told me the guy I was dating at the time was the man of my dreams. He'd turned out to be a nightmare. So much for her intuitive abilities.

"Yes, I know."

"You do?"

He shrugged again. So Italian. "I made some inquiries. I wanted to keep, you know . . . informed. If she comes here, she won't find much of a welcome. In fact, I've offered a reward to the ferryboat captain if he pushes her overboard."

I laughed. His protectiveness over Zeca tickled me.

He glanced away, then back again. "Do you know if she is happy?" He seemed to genuinely want to know.

"I don't know . . . I think she . . ." I sat back in my seat. "She always struck me as somebody who seems so disappointed in life and yet, more than anyone I know, she has done exactly what she wanted to do."

"That's interesting. Toppy told me the same thing." He stood. "What are you going to do with your afternoon? There are some wonderful walks—"

"Antonio, I know you care about Zeca and Alex, and I really do appreciate your concern for me, but I made a deal with Toppy, and I'm going to the café," I said.

"You should rest."

"No. When I rest, I feel sorry for myself."

"You're just like them." He grinned at me. "You'll do well here. Come, I'll walk you down to the café."

We made our way down the millions of steps, and an old lady came running after us.

"Investigatore!" she called out to Antonio. She held two tiny glasses in her hand containing yellow liquid. I soon learned it was homemade limoncello. We each took a glass, toasted each other and told her, "Grazie!"

The drink was delicious. She looked so pleased. She asked after Zeca. Antonio mimed somebody sleeping, and she nodded. "Always working!"

"Not quite," Antonio told me as we reached the terrazza, which was filling up quickly with late lunch goers. "Are you okay if I leave you here?" he asked at the entrance to Café Toppy.

"Sure. I'll be fine. What time is it?"

"Two o'clock. Lunch service is about to start, and then at five, we close up. Zeca and I will be back to help you do that."

"We close at five?"

"Siesta, my friend, only I get mine now." He wiggled his brows. "Zeca and I will take you out to dinner tonight. Toppy opens up about eight."

"That's a question I want to ask. Why did Alex and Zeca tell me I should work lunch and not dinner?"

"Are you serious?" He looked scandalized. "The nighttime is for romance. Toppy's an old man. He takes his romance in the daytime. Besides, when he runs the kitchen at night, he yells too much." He paused. "Don't tell him I said that."

He gave me a cheery wave and vanished.

In the café, a ton of patrons sat, arms folded across their chests, hostile gazes on me that suggested that Toppy's pristine Yelp ratings were about to suddenly plummet.

"I'm a newbie," I announced to them all. "Sorry. I'll be with you shortly." Where was Toppy? Where was . . . anybody? I darted into the kitchen, where I saw two very handsome Eastern European types madly chopping vegetables and chicken.

"You taken any orders yet?" the closest one to me asked.

I gaped at him. "Is that what I'm supposed to do?"

"Well somebody is." He gave me a sullen look. "Unless you think I can read the customers' minds. I could try, but you would be very unhappy with the results."

"Hello?" somebody called from the café.

The kitchen hand lifted a brow at me. "You're the new guy?"

"Yeah."

"The one who disturbed the bread this morning?"

Holy cow. I was never going to live this down.

"That would be me."

"I'm Josip, and this is Alen. We're here for the summer helping Toppy."

"Nice to meet you. I'm Marius."

"Yeah. I saw you all over the Internet this morning," Josip said. "Get busy. The orders don't take themselves."

Aye-aye, captain. Geez. He was worse than Toppy.

I returned to the café in time to see one of the patrons standing behind the counter trying to make his own cappuccino.

"What do you think you're doing?" I screamed at him. He looked at me.

"What am I doing? I think I'm doing your job."

"You can't help yourself," I said. Boy, I was lousier than lousy at this waiting gig. I resolved on the spot to tip all waiters I came across in the future much, much better.

"Yes, I can."

21

When I didn't respond, he said, "I'm Hugh, Alex's boyfriend."

I blinked. "Oh, right. We already met. For a moment I thought you were a customer."

"I *am* a customer. Where's Alex?"

"Don't ask me."

"I *am* asking you."

"I don't know."

"You should take some orders. The customers are looking huffy."

Huffy? Two of them had just risen and were ready to storm out.

"I think they hate me," I whined.

"No problem. Here, let me show you how you handle the tourists." His voice rose. "Ladies and gentlemen, we're sorry for the colossal cock-up today but our new barista is going to take your orders, and there'll be free limoncello for everybody!"

There was a general appreciative murmur.

"The limoncello's in the fridge. Don't tell Toppy," Hugh whispered to me. I nodded, thanked him and spent the next three hours waiting hand and foot on a bunch of tourists who frankly seemed damned snooty to me. I was so busy I hadn't even noticed that Alex had joined me. He made endless coffees, and Hugh and I were handling orders and making cold drinks. We were so crazed, Josip and Alen were rushing out of the kitchen bringing food out to the tables themselves.

I washed more spoons and glasses in those three hours than I had in my whole adult life. I never wanted to see another spoon again. Ever. Then I realized I hadn't done much washing because for twelve years I'd lived off craft services at the studio. I hadn't had to lift a finger, and in my downtime on the weekends, I usually slept in late and skipped breakfast. I often did PR on the weekends, and the studio publicist collected me and always took me to lunch.

I'd opened more boutiques, shops, schools, hospitals, hair salons, halfway homes, crisis centers, sport facilities, and animal shelters than most people had hot dinners.

As I wiped down yet another table, I thought about my life as an actor. I'd been the host of the BAFTA TV Crafts Awards ceremonies three years straight. I'd done every damned thing the studio wanted of me.

And I still hadn't won a bloody BAFTA award . . .

I washed the last of the glasses, feeling more traumatized than I had after the morning rush.

"You'll get used to it," Josip said, sounding kinder than he had earlier. "You picked up the pace, and you only broke nine glasses."

"Thanks."

He waited a moment but didn't seem to know what else to say. I watched him and Alen disappearing out the door, massive backpacks slung on their shoulders.

I left the glasses upside down on a draining cloth and found Hugh and Alex at a table just inside the door. Zeca and Antonio arrived and began closing up.

"Sit down, have a limoncello," Alex urged me.

I sat beside him, and he poured me a glass. It was amazing. Even better than the one the old lady had given me earlier.

"Sorry I was late," Alex said. "We had a slight crisis at the hotel."

"Tell him what happened," Hugh said. He was a handsome man with curly brown hair cut short on the sides, long on top and so attractively that it fell boyishly over his forehead. He had laughing blue eyes and fantastic white teeth. A cosmopolitan British man.

"We had some American film producer check in. He's

been so demanding since the second he arrived. Kept telling me if I didn't do this or that he'd put it on Yelp," Alex said. "We've never had anyone so . . . so obnoxious staying with us before."

"Oh, God. One of those." I rolled my eyes sympathetically. Actually, my whole body ached so badly that even my eyes didn't work properly. They sort of went up and stayed there. I shook my head to loosen them up.

"And then, get this, when he tried going online to blast me, he found the Internet was down. He went berserk. He called the police."

"He didn't!"

Hugh laughed. "And guess who came running?"

"Antonio?" I had to laugh, too. "Boy did he pick the wrong family to mess with."

"Yeah. He told the guy he was an *imbecille*."

"Antonio is such a master of language, isn't he?" I said, making everybody laugh.

Zeca and Antonio dragged chairs over, and we all helped ourselves to more limoncello.

"What happened to your *imbecille* customer?" I asked Alex.

"He got a police escort down to the harbor. He actually didn't realize he was being tossed off the island. He thought he was being treated as somebody special." Alex grinned at the memory. "Ya gotta love dealing with the public."

I reached a hand down to rub my shin bone. I'd kept running into things all afternoon.

"My favorite game is *Diner Dash* but it in no way prepared me for this," I said. The others laughed. "And I understand the spoon thing now, Zeca. Where the hell do they all go?"

"Beats me. Welcome to my nightmare."

We laughed and chatted a little longer, then Antonio said,

"Do you want to rest a bit? Or do you feel like taking in some sights? We thought we'd take you for a walk around the island, then to our favorite pizza place for dinner."

"A walk sounds good. An early dinner." I looked at Zeca. "When do I work again?"

"You'll be working one to five tomorrow. I let you nap a little longer today, but you need to be here to help prepare the lunch service. There are people who come for coffees before two, but lunch isn't served until then."

"Right." I understood now why people had been sitting there waiting. Zeca thought Alex would be there and Alex thought I'd be there.

We washed our glasses and closed the doors on the café. Alex and Hugh walked part of the way with us. "You have to come for dessert at the hotel," Hugh insisted. "Alex makes a great lemon soufflé that our guests go mad over."

"I'd love it."

"We'll be there," Antonio said. We all hugged one another, then I watched Alex and Hugh go off hand in hand. Antonio and Zeca were a little more restrained. I suspected it was because Antonio was a cop. They led me along the main drag, Via Camerelle. Even though it was still sunny, some of the store owners had started turning on shop window lights.

"They do this because they now go for a siesta and when they come back, their windows won't be dark," Antonio explained. "The window shoppers can enjoy all the treasures that await them."

That made sense. I had the feeling the whole island catered to the tourist trade, one way or another. Our pace was slow, and to me, seductive. We had all the time in the world. A luxury for me. When I thought back to my old life, I would return to my apartment around six or seven, usually later. By then it was dark and gloomy, even in summer. Or as we British like to say, *summer, what summer*? I'd swallow down some food I'd popped in the microwave oven and nine times out of ten I'd fall asleep trying to watch an episode of one of my favorite TV shows such as *The Thick of It* or *Miranda*.

I'd awaken on the sofa at two or three o'clock in the morning and trundle off to bed, only to have to wake up at four to be at the studio by five.

Antonio was pointing out a section of the street called Noble Alleyway. I took in the beautiful plants and trees and the ancient stone architecture that made up this little nook in paradise. The stores were all beautiful. I was particularly taken with the upper floors of each one, which all featured window boxes spilling over with colorful flowers, the rooms beyond them looking immaculate and perfect. And already very well lit.

There wasn't a scarf, sandal, or gem out of place anywhere in the windows.

"Businesses do very well here," Antonio told me. "Some of the stores have been here for many generations. Canfora, for example, has been here since nineteen forty-six. There are some ladies who save up all year and return in the summer to buy their sandals."

We came to Augustus Gardens, and I realized Zeca was suddenly emotional.

"This is where we had our first date," he said to Antonio, who reached for his hand.

"I know, bello." Zeca said nothing for a moment. He gazed out to sea. I almost tiptoed away from their private moment, but then Antonio spoke.

"Bello, please don't remember the past. I hate thinking about when I didn't know you."

Zeca nodded. Antonio looked anxious. He glanced up and down the terraced street, saw that nobody was around, and took Zeca's face in his hands and kissed him. I couldn't take my gaze away from this tender yet very passionate moment.

Antonio broke off the kiss. "Come . . . we're making poor Marius feel left out."

Zeca grinned at me. "He's not left out." He kissed my cheek. Antonio kissed the other. They threaded their arms through mine, and we made our way across the piazzetta, another delightful location of outdoor restaurants and exquisite boutiques.

"This is a rich person's paradise, isn't it?" I said. "I mean . . . you wouldn't want to be poor here."

"We get all kinds of travelers," Antonio said. "Backpackers—" He leaned over me and smiled at Zeca. "We met a wonderful Swedish couple backpacking through here, didn't we, mi amore?"

"Yes, we did. Sven saved my feet with his socks. Remember that?"

Antonio began to laugh. "How could I forget? I fell in love with your feet that night."

"Oh, you two have it bad," I said.

"Don't worry." Antonio squeezed my arm. "You will find love here. This is the island of romance, after all."

"It's true." Zeca sighed. "Our Swedish friends, Sven and his wife, Marianna, they've turned out to be our closest friends, apart from Alex and Hugh. We just became godparents to their son. They conceived him on this island."

"What about you two?" I asked. "Any plans for a family?"

"One day," Antonio said. A cloud passed over the conversation.

"What is it?" I asked. "Is something wrong?"

"No." Zeca stopped walking. "Antonio, darling, he may as well know. He is family, after all."

"Know what?" I felt a peculiar tightness in my chest. Antonio released me. "You're not sick are you?" I glanced from one to the other. "If you're sick . . . either of you . . . we can get help—"

"God bless you." Antonio put a hand to my cheek. "No, it's nothing like that, but I'm a cop. I can't marry another man. I make no secret of my love for Zeca, and I wear this." He held up his ring finger that bore a wedding ring. "I am married to him in every way, but right now, I am waiting for a commission back in Naples. I have to be patient and wait."

"You're moving to Naples? But I just got here!"

"The course of legal issues moves very slowly here," Antonio said. "I was a detective and got demoted for tangling with the Camorra. They sent me here to Capri, and now I chase beach balls. I thank God they did though because otherwise, I would never have met the love of my life."

They started smooching again.

"So, Hugh and Alex are getting married?" I asked as soon as they stopped.

"Sure," Zeca said. "In Madrid. Dad's paying for it. Says he's been saving money for years. He's organizing everything." He peered at me through the afternoon sun's harsh rays. "You have to come, too."

"You need sunglasses, bello?" Antonio pulled his out of his pocket and slid them onto Zeca's face. They took my arms again, and we wandered along the cobbled streets.

"I know why it feels so . . . strange," I said, stopping suddenly.

"Why?" Zeca asked.

"No cars. There are no cars on this island!"

Antonio laughed. "Exactly. We walk, the way our ancestors did. Who would like a little limoncello?"

"Me!" we chorused.

They took me to the Belvedere of Tragara, and to me, it was the most gorgeous thing I'd ever seen. Perched on a curve of the mountain dotted by pine trees and beautiful, exotic flowers, it was like something out of a sun-drenched Hollywood film set, complete with lemon blossoms and dizzy bees drunk with the stuff.

Alex and Zeca waited for my reaction.

Our view of the ocean below, the crystal blue waters pounding against ancient cliffs and the Faraglioni Rocks deep in the heart of the ocean touched me in emotional ways I couldn't quite understand.

"It's stunning," I said.

"Emperor Caesar built the first house on the island right here in twenty-nine A.D.," Antonio told me. "You ready to see Alex and Hugh's hotel?"

I nodded eagerly. We walked past some of the most dazzling Italian villas I'd ever seen, and the Certosa di San Giacomo, a Carthusian monastery built in 1363. I could hear chanting from within the ancient stone walls.

"It's beautiful," Antonio agreed, "but we haven't always existed so peacefully here with the monks. During the time of the plague in sixteen fifty-six, so many locals died terrible deaths, but the monks gave nobody refuge. They simply shut their doors."

"That's not very Christian," I said.

"God must have thought so, too, because many of the monks died as well, and the locals, who were understandably upset, just flung their bodies into the sea."

I was trying to imagine such going-ons, but couldn't.

We rounded a corner, and there stood a biscuit-colored building that simply took my breath away. It was Villa Bello, the hotel Alex and Hugh had opened. It was clearly not screaming its existence. I had to carefully look for a small bronze plaque with the name almost hidden behind an umbrella pine.

Wrought iron gates kept the world at bay, but a short ring

of the bell, and I mean an actual bell, brought Alex running. Holding a pitcher filled with lemons, he was so excited to see us he hugged us each in turn. He sloshed liquid, but none of us minded.

He led us inside, pouring us tall glasses of his homemade limonata.

"I make it with lemon, a little pineapple juice, and a dash of pomegranate," he said.

The drink was unbelievable.

"Thanks." He grinned when we all raved. "Soon, I'll put you out on the sundeck where you can watch the gorgeous man parade. But for now, let me show you around."

He handed the jug off to Hugh, who took it outside. I could see men in various stages of undress holding out their glasses for refills.

I was speechless as we passed through an antique-filled lobby that had exquisite tapestries on the walls. Lemons and flowers made up the floral arrangements, and out of the numerous, open glass doors, I spotted some of the hottest guys I'd ever seen in my life lounging around the perfect, heart-shaped pool overlooking the ocean.

Alex told me they had sixteen bedrooms. "This used to be a private residence, so none of the rooms is the same. Ten of them have private spa tubs on their decks. Some have saunas. We have massage therapists and an esthetician for facials, manicures, and pedicures . . . we want this to be the most luxurious vacation any of our guests have ever had."

He showed me around, and even though Zeca and Antonio had been here before, they too seemed mesmerized.

I was staggered at the simple, yet elegant beauty of the place. There wasn't a single unhappy person in residence. Not that I could see. I could imagine how out of place the fraught American producer would have been here.

I saw handsome, sexy men in micro swimsuits walking

hand in hand past us. Man, I was so turned on. Everyone had a smile, a thank you, a gracious word to Alex about their perfect waffles he'd brought to them that morning or the thoughtful gifts he had left in their rooms the previous evening.

"The lemon hand-scrub was something else, my skin is so soft," one man said. I was certain I'd seen him somewhere before, but perhaps that was wishful thinking. I could not get enough of this place, and I loved the peek Alex allowed me into one room being prepared for its latest guest. The double suite had been decorated with all white bedding and pale egg-yolk trim. I was impressed with the soft white leather sofa, love seat and, I was stunned to see in the bedroom, a sex swing dangling from the ceiling.

"A request from our client," Alex said. "He's a regular. A wealthy Italian designer, who comes with a different man each week. He's about sixty and his dates are in their early twenties, but they're captivated by him."

I took in the welcome gift of champagne, fresh island peaches, a box of salted caramels, and matching, teeny tiny, men's, white lace Joe Snyder underpants.

"The style is called Capri. We give it to all our guests," Alex said. I could tell he was enjoying my reactions to everything.

Along the mantelpiece made of stone and decorated with five-hundred-year-old temple mosaics, according to Alex, stood six individual floral designs of twisted willow branches, lemons, and limes. The fireplace below contained fresh logs and I could imagine in the winter months it would get a lot of use.

Antonio, Zeca, and I walked outside onto the huge balcony with its matching white chaises, huge, hide-it-all umbrellas, and bougainvillea-strewn, wrought iron railing that both allowed for some privacy but also an uninterrupted view of the ocean.

Zeca and Alex started kissing again under a beautiful, fragrant wisteria tree.

I caught a glimpse of a man on the balcony next door. Well, next door a few hundred feet away. It was him. The man who'd run past us outside Toppy's. He still wore all black. Long black pants, a zippered black sweater. He was very handsome with jet-black hair. He appeared to be as mesmerized by the view as I was.

He must have sensed me staring because he turned and held my gaze.

"*Buon pomeriggio,*" he said, sounding very Italian. I returned the greeting. He swiftly disappeared inside his room. Drat the luck. I noticed what looked like a penthouse right and high above us. Alex told me it was their best suite. "It's booked out until January two thousand twenty," he said.

"Wow, that's fantastic, Alex."

"It's very special. It has a small private swimming pool and"—he bit his lip—"it has a toy room and, of course, complete and total privacy. It even has its own elevator that only Hugh and I, and the suite's butlers have access to—and our guest, of course."

"Of course." I grinned. "They have butlers?"

"Two. They wait on them hand and foot. The view really is spectacular. The Castiglione hill is so close you can almost reach out and touch it."

"And the toy room doesn't involve Lego, I take it?"

"No." He blushed slightly when the three of us laughed. "You have to understand, we cater to a high flying, very rich, pampered crowd. The guests we have right now wanted butlers who would work only for them." He shrugged. "That's not the strangest request I've ever had."

"What is the strangest request you've ever had?" I asked.

He shook his head. "There was a guy who wanted to bury

his dog's ashes on the property."

I gaped at him. "He brought his dog's ashes to Capri?"

Alex lifted his hands in the Italian way. "He'd always wanted to move here, and he ran into bad luck with his landlady when he finally did move. She wouldn't allow dogs. There's been a lot of bad blood on the island between dog owners and those who hate to step in . . . you know, doggy-do."

"It's become quite contentious," Zeca said. "Every single dog owner on the island's been forced to register their pet's DNA, and any poop that isn't scooped is tested in Naples."

"Are you joking?" I couldn't believe what I was hearing.

"So this poor guy had no place to stay, and I let him come here," Alex said. "He had to go back to Rome after a few days, and his dog, Sunny, evidently died as he was walking him one night. He had him cremated. He begged me to let him bury his ashes here."

"Did you allow him to do it?"

"Yes, I did. Hugh and I felt really bad for him. We loved Sunny, and I think it gave that poor man some comfort. We found him a house to rent in Anacapri, and I think he's happy now. He adopted a cute little dog in Naples . . . and planted a rose bush over Sunny's ashes right here in our garden. They come and visit him every week." He grinned. "That's the only place the new pup doesn't pee on when he comes here."

"What about Mr. Ferrari?" Antonio asked.

"Oh, yeah. This guy wanted me to take him to buy a Ferrari, but they don't allow cars on the island. I arranged for him to buy one in Rome. Dad actually went with him."

"What about Mr. Angles?" Zeca looked like he wanted to laugh.

"Oh my, how could I forget Mr. Angles?" Alex shook his head. "He was a weirdo. He emailed me asking about what

33

angle the sun set on each room. I had no idea. I had to ask around to find a mathematician who could pinpoint the exact degree to which each room's sunsets were angled—have you ever heard of such a thing?"

I shook my head.

"Well, I know now." He chuckled. "I know all the angles for each season. Our client picked the room he wanted based on this single point, and I guess he was pleased. He's already booked again for the same time next year."

"You really go out of your way to give them their dream vacations," I said. I was very impressed.

"Of course. We try to cater to all our clients' deepest desires."

"I feel so . . . boring," Antonio said. "All I want is a nice room, a breeze, and my Zeca."

"You? Boring? Never." Zeca snuggled into him.

Alex's cell phone vibrated. He checked the readout. "I have to get to the kitchen. Why don't you all go sit by the pool? I'll bring you some aperitifs and a few hors d'oeuvres."

We took his suggestion, and I relaxed on a well-padded chaise as the late afternoon sun caressed my skin.

Zeca and Antonio shared another chaise, Zeca leaning back against Antonio's chest and belly. We all kicked off our shoes. A very cute waiter in white shorts and a crisp, sleeveless shirt brought us limoncello in frosted, square apéritif glasses. We all wanted refills on the limonata, too, so he returned with the jug. I glanced up to thank him and saw the tall man in the black track pants watching us. As soon as I caught his gaze, he moved away from the balcony.

Whatever . . .

I checked back in with Antonio and Zeca's conversation. They were talking about Alex's flair for Italian street cooking.

"Wait until you try his food," Zeca said.

"I can't wait. This is the life," I said. "I could get used to it."

"You will." Antonio turned and chuckled. "This is Capri."

I was so glad I'd come now. I could smell figs, lemon, and rosemary from the trees and plants around us. The roar of the ocean, the clean breeze, my cousins' happiness . . . it was all conspiring to make me smile like they did. The island's magic was starting to become contagious. Something made me glance up at the balcony again. There was the man in the black track pants. Once more he turned and seemed to flee.

Alex returned with a laden silver tray. I heard the chorus of approvals around us. He let his paying guests take his little treats first, then he came to us.

I sat up a little straighter and looked at the tiny, fluffy bread rolls that made two perfect bites. Oh . . . food to be shared.

"This is homemade bread with shrimp and arugula, a tiny bit of mayo with chives and a squeeze of lemon." Alex mimed, squeezing a lemon over the food.

I picked up a wedge and swallowed mine quickly. The shrimp was zesty and fresh. The combination of tastes and textures made my spirits soar.

Next, he brought us tiny pizzas the size of dollar pancakes. I had never tasted anything like these in my life. They were made with feta cheese, pistachio nuts, fresh thyme, and drizzled with a homemade apricot dressing.

Holy heck. I could die now and go to heaven extremely happy.

Alex kept bringing little bites that had everyone on the terrace sitting up straight waiting for more. Three small but succulent pieces of lamb, interspersed with baked brie and arugula on lemongrass spears came next.

Limoncello kept flowing. I was getting tipsy.

"I want to go home and fuck," Zeca suddenly announced.

"You won't get an argument from me, but we promised Marius dinner," Antonio said. "Besides, I'm not sure my legs will cooperate."

Zeca signed and snuggled back into his lover's body. "Let's just stay here. We can talk Alex into making us pizza."

"How do you feel about that?" Antonio asked me.

"Sounds good to me," I said. I couldn't resist adding, "*Dolce far niente.*"

He grinned at me. "Isn't it though? How sweet it is to do nothing."

We lay back on our chaises, the sun starting its descent into the sea. I might have fallen asleep had Alex not coming racing out to us, running up to Antonio.

"You have to come quick," he said. He glanced around, trying to keep his voice low.

"What is it?" Antonio's urgency matched his as he sat up on the chaise.

"Something that's never ever happened before." Alex choked back tears. "We've had a robbery. One of our guests has been burglarized."

CHAPTER THREE

The three of us sobered up fast. Zeca and Antonio stuffed their feet back into their shoes. Zeca went off to the kitchen to replace Alex, who led Antonio to the burgled suite.

I didn't know what to do with myself. I sat on my chaise and waited. What an awful thing . . . I hoped it was a mistake. The sun wanted to lull me to sleep, but I thought, tired as I was, it would be rude to drift off during a family crisis. I struggled to stay awake, and a few minutes later, Antonio came back out, beckoning me.

"You should come with me," he said, his tone reluctant.

"Me?" I couldn't imagine why. I put my running shoes back on and followed him.

"This has never happened at all here in Capri," Antonio muttered. "The biggest crime I've had to investigate in the past year is doggie DNA. That's my professional life these days. Puppy poopies and missing beach balls."

We rounded a corner. "You get a lot of missing beach balls?"

"Yes." He sounded aggrieved. "And sometimes I get the beach balls that have fallen in the poop—" He stopped when we encountered a frantic-looking Alex.

"Alex, please alert the front desk not to let anyone leave the premises until I've had a chance to speak to the victim. Whatever's been stolen, this was an inside job."

"I—" Alex looked pale, but he quickly texted the front desk from his cell phone. When he led us to a room right near where I'd seen the man in the black sweatpants, I wondered whether I should mention him to Antonio, but as soon as we walked in, there he was.

He'd been pacing, his hands on his slim, elegant hips, but he stopped as soon as he saw us.

"Did you call me and ask me to meet you?" He jabbed a finger at me.

"Me?" I blinked like a fool. Antonio stepped in with smooth words that would have calmed anyone.

"Signore Alvarenga, as I said a few moments ago, Marius is new to the island, and I can vouch for the fact he hasn't made a single call since we came into the hotel."

The man in black was angry but trying very hard to disguise it. He kept pacing, glaring at me. I couldn't understand why he thought I'd called him.

Alex moved across the room to him. "Signore Alvarenga, I must apologize once more. My brother-in-law, Detective Moretti, will investigate this matter fully, I promise you."

"Please, call me Crisanto." The man seemed less hostile now. He gazed at Antonio. "I had a feeling you were the hot detective everyone talks about." He reached over and shook his hand.

Antonio's cheeks flushed. "Signore Alvarenga—"

"Crisanto to you, too," the man told Antonio, who seemed to have to tug a little extra hard to get his fingers out of Crisanto's grip. Now I'd heard the man saying a few more words I knew he wasn't Italian. Was he Spanish? No . . . not Spanish. *Something more exotic*, I thought. *Argentina? Venezuela?*

My God, he is gorgeous. I want to eat his accent on toast. With butter.

Antonio nodded. "Okay, Crisanto. I just want to say I am a fan. A big fan."

The man smiled. His anger seemed to have evaporated. Who was he?

"Grazie," he said.

Up close he was a specimen. I'd never seen anyone so lithe, so . . . catlike. He had an easy grace, a contained energy that I found intimidating, yet very alluring. The caramel sheen to his skin perfectly housed his muscular but not pumped-up build.

He looked right at me. "I know I have seen you somewhere, but I don't know where."

I blushed. Alex introduced us. "This is my cousin, Marius Treadway."

Crisanto kept staring at me as we shook hands, obviously still trying to place me. I was doing the same thing.

Who is he that Antonio is such a fan?

For a guy who'd just been robbed, he was actually being very pleasant. I hung back and let Antonio take control. It took me a moment to realize I probably should just slip away now that he'd accepted that I hadn't called him, but I thought drawing more attention to myself probably wasn't a good idea.

"Crisanto, can you tell me what has been taken and approximately when this happened?" Antonio asked.

"Yes. My wallet. Not my money wallet. I have a black leather billfold. It's a British one . . . .ah . . . Ettinger. It has my passport, both of them actually. I have one from Brazil and an EU one."

Brazil . . . no wonder he's so yummy . . .

"What color is the Brazilian passport?" Antonio jotted notes on a small notepad he'd taken out of his pocket.

"Burgundy. Very similar to the European passport. It's so frustrating. I just renewed my driver's license, and that was in there, too. I can't travel, I can't do anything without identification. I start training for the first soccer match of the season in Genoa this weekend. I cannot miss it."

"I understand," Antonio soothed. "Where did you last see the wallet?"

"On my bed. I left everything here and went to the roof terrace because somebody called my room and said there were cocktails there."

"Somebody called you and said that?" Alex looked shocked. "Somebody in this hotel?"

"I thought so." Crisanto shrugged. He fixed me with a momentary glance but looked away again. "When I came back, my door was still open—"

"You left it open?" Antonio asked.

"Yes." Crisanto shot him a defiant glance. "This island is supposed to be so safe, isn't it?"

"It is." Antonio moved back toward the door. "So you went out, left the door open, and the wallet on the bed?"

"Yes. I was very thirsty."

"But I left a bottle of Cristal and several bottles of mineral water for you, per your request," Alex said. "I even put in an extra bottle of Cristal with our compliments."

"Shit," Crisanto said. His hands were on his hips again, and he stomped his foot on the floor. He blew out a breath. "I thought it was him calling me like I said."

Alex and Antonio stared at me. I shrugged. Antonio had a look of amusement in his eyes.

"I'm curious about why you thought Marius was calling you?"

Crisanto's gaze narrowed. "We noticed each other . . . earlier. Outside that café."

Alex and Antonio looked surprised. Crisanto's eyes went black as his gaze seared into mine.

Oh, my . . .

My cock hardened. That was inappropriate. So inappropriate. I tried to tell my nether regions this, but they screamed back at me . . . *Free willy! Free willy!*

"And then I saw him looking at me from the other balcony earlier. We exchanged greetings. And then when my phone rang . . ." He shrugged.

I felt rather bouncy at this point.

Crisanto Alvarenga had seen me and was attracted to me. I tried not to show my obvious glee. The man had been robbed, after all.

"Crisanto, is that the only thing that was taken?" Antonio asked.

"Yes, my other wallet with money and credit cards is in my pocket."

Antonio nodded. "I'm going to dust the door for prints and . . ." He looked at Alex. "Can you check the upstairs terrace, please, just in case?"

Alex left the room immediately. Crisanto sounded really annoyed when he said, "Look, I left it on the bed, I tell you."

"When you went up to the terrace, you realized there were no cocktails, and what did you do then?" Antonio asked.

"I came back down here, of course. I called the front desk. They knew nothing of cocktails upstairs. They said they could have one brought to me. I told them I just needed more towels and then I realized my billfold was missing."

One of the room maids showed up, looking nervous. She was carrying the stack of pale blue towels that apparently Crisanto had requested.

"Grazie," Antonio said, taking them from her. He looked at Crisanto as he dumped the towels on top of the pale blue bedspread.

"I need to return to the station to get my crime scene kit."

"Look! Look!" Alex came flying back into the room, a black leather billfold in hand.

"That's it!" Crisanto looked stunned.

"Where was it?" Antonio asked.

"Near the balcony doors upstairs."

"But I—" Crisanto grabbed it from Alex's fingers and examined the contents. "All here. I have a U.S. hundred-dollar bill tucked into one of the panels. That's still here, too."

He looked embarrassed. "I swear, I did not take this thing upstairs."

"Well, I'm glad you found it now and that everything's okay," Alex said. "Will you accept dinner here tonight as our guest?"

"I—no, I don't know. I'm supposed to go out. I suppose everything is okay . . . Thanks for finding it, but I want you to know, this billfold did not leave this room in my hand."

"I'm very sorry," Alex said. "Is there anything I can get for you?"

"No. Thanks. This has been very stressful." Crisanto's earlier pleasantness evaporated. "I don't know what to think." He let out a breath. "Please don't get your crime scene kit. I want to forget this happened. I'm just relieved I got my identification back."

"I understand and, once again, I am sorry this happened to you," Antonio said.

Crisanto said nothing. We left the room when it became obvious that he was getting more and more upset and that he wanted to be left alone.

Down the corridor, we looked at each other.

"What do you think?" Antonio asked, his voice low.

I shook my head. "I think somebody took his wallet and dumped it when they realized—or thought—there was no money or credit cards in it."

"Me, too." Antonio looked at Alex. "What do you think?"

"I'm inclined to agree." Alex sounded worried. "It's not good. This is the second catastrophe today. We've never had two incidents like this the whole time we've been open, let alone in a single day."

We went down to the kitchen. Alex relieved Zeca, who looked concerned.

"It's all over the kitchen that the great Crisanto got

42

robbed," he said. "The room service staff members are worried that one of them will be blamed."

"How did it get out?" Antonio wanted to know.

"He came to the front desk yelling and screaming when he first realized his wallet was missing," Alex said. "I asked him to let me consult you." He looked very upset now. "I should have listened to your suggestion that we have a security guard on staff. Do you think your friend in Naples might still be interested?"

"Sure," Antonio said. "I think it's a very good idea. Listen . . . are there any new members of staff working here?"

"None," Alex said. "And you know Hugh, and I screened everyone carefully."

"Do you want us to stay for dinner?" Antonio asked.

"God, yes. Zeca, thanks for pinch-hitting in the kitchen."

"No problem, sweetie. I can still give you a hand."

"No way. I want you, Antonio, and Marius to grab a table on the terrace. We're about to have some musical entertainment." He looked on the verge of tears. "Maybe I should have mentioned it but . . ." His voice trailed away. His face crumpled in grief.

"What is it?" Zeca grabbed his brother and hugged him.

"We've had some . . . funny emails."

"What kind of emails?" Antonio asked.

"Threats." Alex allowed his brother to fuss over him a moment.

"I want to see them." Antonio's face looked thunderous. The three of us went into the office that Alex shared with Hugh. He had printouts of the emails.

"Why didn't you tell me about these earlier?" Antonio's tone was deadly.

"I didn't take them seriously." Alex looked defeated. "Whoever is behind this . . . he'll ruin us!"

"Do you know me at all?" Antonio asked. He put his free hand on Alex's shoulder. "I'm not going to let anyone hurt you."

"No, he won't Alex. And neither will I," Zeca said.

"And neither will I." I had to blink back tears. Alex was so distraught.

"I need to get into your emails," Antonio said. Alex's laptop was already turned on, and Antonio got busy. "Both of these were sent from an account in Naples." Antonio kept typing.

"Whoever sent them tried using proxy addresses, but he is an idiot."

Antonio had left the two printouts on Alex's desk.

"May I look at them?" I asked.

"Sure." Alex handed them to me. I was shocked at the vicious tone to them.

Owners of Hotel Bello, you are sick scum. Close your doors or else.

That was the first one.

The second one said,

I gave you a warning. You chose to ignore it. Close the hotel, or I'll close it for you! Fags!

"Wow," I said.

"I know, right?" Alex nodded. "Somebody who is here in the hotel is trying to ruin us!"

"Well, we assume these incidents are all linked," Antonio said. "Since the emails were both sent last week, we would be foolish not to think there's a connection. I just forwarded them to my own account. I am going to trace the ISPs listed . . . whoever sent these used a free, public proxy. Hide My Ass is the company and they fold like a pack of cheap cards when pushed. Believe me, I will push, and the idiot behind all this will wish he'd hidden his ass better."

He stood. "And now, we'll have a little dinner, then I've got to get to work. I just sent an email to my friend, Ibrahim.

I'll see how quickly he can start working for you. In the meantime, I'm going to be spending a lot of time here."

"Wonderful!" Alex looked happier already.

"Until Ibrahim can get here, I'll just work out of this office if that's okay with you, Alex."

Alex looked overjoyed. "Okay? It's fantastic. Can't I pay you to stay here forever?"

Antonio gave him a disarming smile. "No, but you can try bribing me with lemon soufflé."

Alex grinned. He rushed off to his kitchen, and the three of us went out to the pool area. There was a relaxed, happy vibe that hadn't been destroyed in spite of the ugly incident.

"Who does Crisanto play for?" I asked Antonio as we sipped fresh cocktails.

"Really? You don't know?"

"He plays for Genoa," Zeca said quickly.

"I didn't know . . . I don't follow Italian football."

"There was a big war over him. Milan wanted him . . . lots of people wanted him, but Genoa's having an exciting season and we think he's going to pull the club back to the top of Serie A."

"Well . . . he's sure sexy enough."

Two seconds later, he was hovering by my shoulder. I wondered if he'd heard me. Color crept up my face. I hadn't blushed like this since my first pre-teen crush.

"Hello again," he said. "Am I disturbing you all?"

"No," Zeca said. He and Antonio got up quickly and arranged a chair for him right beside me. I don't know who was more embarrassed, Crisanto or I, but the awkward moment passed when Alex came out with a platter bearing a huge, fragrant mound of bread.

My mouth began watering.

"I've been slow cooking this all day in honor of Crisanto," Alex said. "It's a bread only made in Genoa, it's called a *fugassa*, and he insisted on sharing it with you all."

"Oh!" the three of us said in unison. Nothing could have made us happier.

"It looks like the real thing," Crisanto enthused. "I buy this there . . . it smells like the real thing, too."

Alex handed him a knife, then placed three different types of olive oil on the table for dipping. "This one is pure olive oil, this is infused with lemon, and the last one is rosemary. Ciao!"

He darted off, and Crisanto began cutting. I'd never tasted bread with such a succulent center. It was crispy on the outside, almost sweet inside. I didn't want to dilute the flavor with any of the oils, but Crisanto insisted.

"The lemon oil is my favorite." He picked up the bottle and poured a little on my plate. He was right, if anything, it enhanced the flavor.

"So you live in Genoa?" I asked.

He smiled. "Yes. And you? You're English, aren't you?"

"But I live here now." I had my eye on the bread again. "It's sort of like focaccia only better," I said as Crisanto hacked me another slice.

"You are right." Antonio mumbled around his own piece. "Genovese bread is the origin of the humble focaccia."

"Someday I'd like to drive all around Italy with you and make you show me all the little places that make these wonderful foods," Zeca said.

"And I'll take you." Antonio covered Zeca's free hand with his.

"When Antonio and I went to Naples together the first time he introduced me to fried pizza," Zeca announced. "I still dream about that stuff."

"Oh, it's good!" Crisanto nodded enthusiastically. "It has a special taste all of its own. Do you think Alex will be making his fried ravioli tonight?"

"I hope so," Antonio said.

Their food conversation was making me get whiplash as I took in each of their comments.

Alex came back to the table, Hugh in tow.

"Fried ravioli three ways," he said. "This one has crab, caught fresh today, this one has pumpkin and sage, and it's delicious dipped in this honey butter sauce, and the third one is sausage and pancetta."

We all moaned our appreciation. Hugh put a huge salad on the table and began tossing it, putting it into bowls, which we shared around the table.

The musicians who'd been on a break returned, and I noticed a couple of guys getting up to dance.

"Who wants wine?" Hugh asked. He glanced at me. "Another cocktail?"

"I'm fine, thanks. I would love some mineral water though, please."

"Me, too," the others chorused.

Hugh came over to me. "There's a British couple over there, see by the umbrellas? They're big fans. They're wondering if they can have their picture taken with you." He glanced at Antonio. "It's okay, they are not paparazzi."

I stifled a groan. I just wanted to sit and stuff my face, but I smiled and stood, Crisanto rising as I did. That surprised me. He walked over with me and shook hands with the couple, who were very sweet and actually recited entire chunks of my dialogue with me. Fans of *The Fletchers* always surprise me. They come out with the most amazing stuff. You never knew what aspects of the show they liked best.

They were sure quick to tell you when they didn't like something, however.

"I hope they're not killing you off," one of them said, as Hugh dutifully took a couple of photos of the three of us together with each of their cameras.

"The triplets need their father," another guy added.

That shocked me.

"You have triplets?" Crisanto looked agog at me.

"They're mutants," I reminded the fan who went on and on about how the triplets deserved love, even if they were the result of genetic lab experiments.

"I know they are all part lion, monkey, humans, and alien beings, but there's a cure for all of these things. I know a doctor who is doing great research into children's diseases. I can put you in touch with him."

"They're fictional characters, but . . . thank you."

"Fictional characters need love, too," he said. I almost burst out laughing. We all shook hands. Hugh ran off to his kitchen I supposed, and Crisanto and I walked back to join Antonio and Zeca.

"You have . . . mutant children . . . but not real ones? This is on a TV show?" he asked.

"Yes."

"Is it a comedy?"

"No. A soap opera."

"Which one?"

"*The Fletchers.*"

"That's where I've seen you! When I was in London playing a charity football match, you were gang-raped in the hospital. You were really good!"

"Thanks."

"So they killed you off?"

"I've been on it twelve years. I begged them to put me out of my misery."

"Oh, but the poor triplets!" He said this with such sincerity that I was surprised to catch the cheeky grin on his face.

We looked at each other and laughed.

Back at the table, the others had demolished a good portion of the food, but more came out of the kitchen.

Crisanto excused himself for a moment and wandered away.

"Do you like him?" Zeca immediately asked. "He likes you, I can tell."

"You have to date him. I bet you he gives you free tickets to all of his games," Antonio said.

I laughed.

When Crisanto returned, we debated the three dessert options Alex came over and presented to us. We all wanted the lemon soufflé, but I was also about to burst.

"Good thing I'm not staying here, or I'd soon be the size of a tugboat," I said.

The others laughed.

"Tugboats are attractive," Crisanto insisted. He grinned at me. "Can I talk you into having dessert and coffee on my terrace?"

"You won't have to twist my arm." I'm not stupid.

I caught Zeca giving me a discreet thumbs-up as I stood to leave the table with Crisanto.

"Wait—the check." I reached into my wallet.

"No, dinner's on us, remember?" Antonio said. He and Zeca rose and hugged us both. I'd never felt so happy . . . not for a long time, anyway.

On Crisanto's private terrace, away from the crowd, I could still hear the Italian guitarist performing a stirring rendition of some song that I recognized but couldn't place. Crisanto led me to a small table that had flickering candles in tiny jars. There was a knock at the door.

My host made sure I was seated before he left the terrace and returned with Alex, who was beaming when he saw me. He had a laden tray that he quickly emptied. He gave us a pot of coffee and two cups that matched the blue motif of what I'd seen of the soccer player's room. Alex placed a lemon soufflé on the table with two spoons and a variety of sauces and toppings.

"This one is raspberry, made with fresh fruit. This is vanilla and lemon curd ice cream, which is delicious placed right on the middle of the soufflé, and I brought fresh cream. There's also warm chocolate sauce and a passion fruit one if you prefer those." He deposited milk and sugar on the table and then vanished.

"Which sauce do you want?" Crisanto asked me. I was pleased that we both seemed to like the idea of the ice cream, fresh raspberry sauce, and he topped off the concoction with whipped cream.

He dug his spoon into the mixture. Sauce oozed over the edges of the ramekin. Crisanto held the spoon to my lips and fed me. I was a little surprised he didn't follow up with a kiss, but he went on in this manner, feeding me, then himself, pointing out little things for me to look at. Tiny flowers budding on his terrace.

"They will bloom tomorrow. I've been here two days and noticed that the ones getting ready to bloom call out to me," he said.

He poured us coffee. I acted insanely stupid in his company. I worried about holding a cup of coffee and spilling it all over him. I was glad he fed me. Left to my own devices that soufflé would find its way up my nose. He had an intensity that I had noticed the moment we met, but now we were alone, it felt quite . . . expository. I felt like he could read my mind, my body . . .

"Why are you afraid of me?" he suddenly asked.

I shook my head. "Afraid of myself, I think."

He smiled. "Good answer. You feel vulnerable."

"Sure I do. You're gorgeous."

"I'm glad you think so."

I sat back in my chair. I needed a breather. From food, his endless, probing eyes, and my own emotions.

"You've been hurt," he said.

"Who hasn't?" I didn't mean to snap, but I did.

"I don't want to spoil our evening."

"Neither do I. I'm sorry." I shrugged. "I only arrived this morning and the last few weeks haven't been fun."

"Tell me about them."

I broke the cardinal rule of dating. Rule number one: Don't spill your guts on the first date. Well, technically speaking, this wasn't a date, but I let my freak flag fly as I told him about Greece, about Paolo, and why I was here.

"This . . . Paolo . . . he's an actor you said?"

I squinted at him in the encroaching darkness. "Yes."

"Two actors together can't be good."

I nodded. "You're right. He had a career, I did too, and when we were both working it was great, but then his work dried up, and he became very unhappy. He got an offer to do a movie in Los Angeles, and I thought it was the perfect opportunity. And so did he. He broke up with me."

"How long ago was this?"

"Six months ago."

"No chance you will get back together?"

"No. None. What about you?"

He looked at me over the rim of his coffee cup. "I don't get . . . seriously involved. I haven't for a long time."

"That's good to know."

"I have to be discreet," he said. "They don't worship gay soccer players in Europe."

"Or many other places. I know all about discreet."

He nodded. "I know you do. I Googled you a little while ago."

"When? Oh . . . when you left the table?"

He grinned. "You are very discreet. Nothing personal or private at all. The only personal thing I saw was a photo of you working in your uncle's restaurant today. The photographer tried to make it look like you are down on your luck already."

"Yeah . . . well. It could have been worse. He could have photographed my apartment building in Athens."

"Fame is a funny thing, isn't it?"

"Yeah. It's worse for you, I'm sure."

He eyed me with curiosity. "Why do you say that?"

"I get to hide behind a character. People talk about him, not me. I got to know David Beckham, who is not only a brilliant soccer player, but one of the most genuine people I've ever met, and when he signed with Galaxy in Los Angeles, the fans canceled their tickets when he broke his leg and couldn't play."

"Yes," he admitted. "You're right. The weight of expectation is difficult. I'm nervous about my first season with Genoa." His shoulders suddenly sagged. "They had a bad season last time, with one really awful match where the fans threw things at them on the field. I dread that happening to me."

"They won't. You'll deliver."

He just looked at me. Oops. Now I sounded like I expected big things from him, too.

Crisanto shifted in his seat. "People hold you to a high standard, too. Tonight, that man criticized your parenting skills."

I laughed. "Yeah. I get that a lot. It's amazing. People really care about the characters on TV shows. It all stops though. All the love. I was still on air in England last week, and three days later the BBC told me the fan mail, the baby clothing . . . it all stopped arriving."

"Did that bother you?" He put his cup down and leaned toward me.

"No. It was a reminder that it isn't real. I appreciate the fans of the show. The viewers kept me employed. I have always been nice to them. I've always signed autographs, posed for pictures, even if I am in the chemist to fill a prescription for a raging fever, I do it." I looked at him. "That's why I say it's worse for you. Soccer fans are like . . . rabid dogs."

"Yes, they are. Sometimes I find it a bit . . . frightening. People send weird gifts to the soccer club."

"I've had those, too."

"It's not new behavior though," he said. "Fans love hard. Very hard. You know, in six-hundred and twenty BC, Draco, a Greek law-maker, showed up at a theater one night and was smothered to death by gifts of cloaks showered upon him by his appreciative citizens."

That made me laugh. "Cloaked to death."

"Yes." His face clouded for a moment. "I think that's what I'm afraid of. Being cloaked to death. People have so much . . . like you said . . . expectation. I focus so hard on staying in shape, giving soccer my best. Genoa spent a lot of money on me, as the newspapers and the stupid bloggers never fail to remind me." There was more than a trace of bitterness in his tone.

"So is that why you . . . stay single? Is it just your career?"

He reached a hand out to me. "No. I think you figured it out. Like you, I guard my heart."

When he pulled me to my feet and put his arms around me, I was aware of two things. We were both hard, and our hearts were pounding. The third thing I noticed was that he was an amazing kisser, damn him. He made me sweat. The hair at the base of my neck grew damp.

"I would like to invite you to lie down on the bed with me," he said. "I would like to say we don't have to do anything, but it would be a lie." He kissed me again. "I want to show you my whole bag of tricks."

Tricks?

That just hit me all wrong. I knew I should step back. I

should turn and walk away. There is a moment in every budding relationship where a person has to stop and decide if they move forward. Do you feel scared and bolt, or feel scared and still do it? He'd already told me he didn't do 'serious.' Now he was telling me it was tricks. *Razzle, dazzle. Smoke and mirrors.*

I'd had enough of all that. Twelve years on a TV show. I'd made a career of pretense. I'd given it up in pursuit of truth. I didn't want to try to win over another man who was emotionally unavailable.

Walk away, Marius.

It was so damned hard. The devil on my shoulder wanted this man's tongue on my skin. *Show me your tricks! All of them!*

I had enough wherewithal to actually smile and make a joke of it.

"Tricks?" I shook my head. "Here's one for you. Watch me do my disappearing act." I stood on tiptoe and kissed his cheekbone, the right one that had a tiny scar I'd noticed earlier. I'd already developed a little crush on it.

"Thank you for a magical evening and don't let the cloaks crush you." I walked away. I thought I was brilliant, clever, funny, and yet my vulnerability was right there. He didn't respond and didn't follow me.

I didn't expect him to.

Down at the front desk I asked for Alex or Hugh.

"They're having a private meeting," the concierge said. He threw a worried glance at the closed office door.

"Can you tell them that their cousin, Marius, is heading home?"

"Okay." He gave me a weird look. "Are you the one from the TV show?"

"Um. Yeah. I guess that's me."

He nodded. "Some photographer called looking for you."

I was so surprised I didn't know what to say. I settled for,

54

"Thanks for letting me know."

"We told him to bug off." The concierge gave me a huge grin.

That made me laugh. "An extra big thank you."

I left the hotel, and as I walked down the street, I realized I had no idea how to get home. How did I find the spot with the gazillion stairs?

It was dark now, and I'd lost track of time . . . but I had my cell phone. I pulled it out of my pocket. Not so late, ten o'clock. The island was lit up by lights that twinkled all the way down to the harbor. I debated calling Uncle Toppy but being lost was nowhere near the scale of the house being on fire. I could Google his address I supposed but didn't actually know the address. I could walk to the café . . . or would it be closed? I called, but the phone, as usual, rang out.

If I called him at his girlfriend's house would I kill her bread entirely?

I sighed. I was so damned tired. It had been a long day. I kept walking. Zeca. Maybe I could call him, or would he be in bed with Antonio?

Ahead of me, I spotted a man crouching across the street near a bush, adjusting goggles on his face. I'd worn similar ones on the show once. I knew they were night-vision goggles. I peered in the semi-darkness as he spread a neatly manicured hedge apart with his fingers and looked down over another terrace.

"Antonio?" I asked. The hot island cop jumped three feet into the air, clutched his chest, and peered over the hedge again.

"Marius . . . what are you doing sneaking up on me?"

I could tell he was trying hard to hide his annoyance.

"I'm trying to get home. I'm lost. What are you doing here?"

"The mayor says I'm not doing enough to trap the bastard

who keeps doing this." He held up right up near my face two stinky baggies with dog shit inside them.

"Eww!"

"I'm trying to catch the person before the crime lab tests the samples. I have to send them in tomorrow. I'm worried, Marius. First the doggies, now the hotel is having problems."

"You can't take it personally."

He looked affronted. "I take it very personally. If I don't solve these crimes, soon I'll be lucky to be chasing even a beach ball."

"Nah. Everyone on the island loves you."

That seemed to cheer him up. I saw him straighten a little as we came to a cute little house tucked into the mountainside. "You can stay with us tonight," he offered.

"You live here?" It was gorgeous.

"Yes. We have a sofa. Very comfortable. Just ask Toppy. When he's too drunk to get up the stairs to his house, he stays here." He unlocked the front door, and my naked cousin came running. Antonio grinned, but Zeca freaked and ran back through the house.

"See what I have to come home to?" Antonio got a lusty look on his face. "He is my sanity."

He opened a black bag on the dining table and slipped the dog poop samples inside.

He stashed the case in the bathroom to our right, washed his hands, and showed me around. The adorable house was filled with Italian artwork, antiques, and gorgeous glassware.

"Some of these have been handed down to me by my family, and some I collected myself," he told me. "Until Zeca came into my life I didn't really appreciate them. Now I enjoy wine in nice glasses that have a history to them." He gestured toward some grape-colored fluted stem glasses that were simply stunning. The cut facets in them glinted as I held them up. Crystal.

I noticed a tray with six Pittilon wine glasses on their beautiful, seventeenth-century oak credenza. I knew the etching around the rims of the Italian wine glasses was fourteen-carat gold.

Zeca came out with a towel around his waist. "Sorry." He still seemed to be blushing. I pointed to the wine glasses.

"These are stunning."

Antonio grinned. "A gift from our neighbors. They were moving back to Paris and were worried the glasses wouldn't make it. This way they know when they come back for a visit, they have a place to stay and their glasses will be here waiting for some champagne."

The two men gave me a towel and a toothbrush.

Zeca assured me the couch was very comfortable and hastily threw some sheets on it. "We have a spare room, but it's filled with Mama's things."

"Mama?"

His face glowed. "Antonio's mother. She is amazing. Wait until you meet her. She comes and cooks at the café one week a month."

I hugged my cousin. Growing up without a mother must have been awful.

"I'll make you breakfast in the morning, and you can relax a little before your lunch shift," he said.

"Bed now, Zeca," Antonio said.

"I'm coming, sweetie." He turned back to me. "And I'll tell you how to get home so you can shower and change."

"Zeca." Antonio's warning tone turned into a growl. He whipped off Zeca's towel, bent forward, and shouldered my cousin's body. Zeca laughed, kicking his legs. "Oh, my God . . . Antonio!"

Then they were gone. I could have taken a shower. I could

have watched TV or called my parents and told them where I was. I could have picked up one of Zeca's Spanish language books that were crammed onto the overflowing bookshelf.

Instead, I stripped down to my underwear. I fell asleep, dreaming about tricks, and Crisanto Alvarenga.

And what might have been . . .

CHAPTER FOUR

I awoke to the smell of French toast and coffee and sat up. I adore French toast. Antonio was talking, but not in the room. I swiveled around and found Zeca perched on a wing chair, cup of coffee in hand, watching the morning news on a small TV. It wasn't one of the plasma or flat screen kind everybody in England covets; it was an older model, quite fitting for the couple's decor.

"Good morning!" Zeca's eyes shone. "My baby's on TV!"

"Turn it up," I said. Antonio and some guy in an ill-fitting suit were holding a press conference. "Is that the *terrazzina*?"

Zeca nodded. "Doesn't he look handsome in his teal shirt?"

He did. Antonio commanded the screen in his shirt that matched the color of the Capri sky. He stood, hands on hips, sunglasses on, every bit the macho movie spy.

"We have now collected the DNA of all the dogs on this island," the guy in the suit beside him said.

"That's the mayor," Zeca told me. "A real tool." He rushed off to bring me a cup and the coffee pot.

"This is a small island. It is ten square miles all the way around, and there are seven thousand, five hundred residents and one thousand dogs," the mayor said. "Some of the walkways are ancient and very narrow, and some of our residents are elderly. For some of them, trying to pick their way down the street is like doing a slalom down a tricky mountainside."

Zeca and I burst into laughter.

"Ooh, I shouldn't laugh," he whispered dramatically. "The old lady two houses over fell on the street and broke her hip. She bugs Antonio constantly to find the poopy offender."

The mayor spoke both in Italian and English. He kept going back and forth. He had a smooth, confident manner.

"We want to keep Capri beautiful. We want to keep Capri safe," he went on. "Together with Detective Moretti here, and his staff, we have maintained a zero crime rate." He held up his fingers to make a zero. "And a zero tolerance for dog poop! Each sample we find is being sent to a crime lab in Naples, and the owners of these dogs will be fined."

The reporters surrounding him started firing off questions.

"Wasn't it a stroke of brilliance?" Zeca sighed. "Antonio suggested this impromptu press conference. He thought it would give the mayor the chance to hog the limelight—and deflect attention from the incidents at the hotel yesterday."

I nodded. The reporters were asking about dog poop and the cost of fines. It was so hard not to laugh.

"Any suspects?" one of them asked.

"That's classified," Antonio said a small smile on his lips.

"Classified!" Zeca and I howled in unison.

"That was brilliant," I said. "Who do you think it is?"

"No idea. He's out there every night but no luck so far." He glanced at me. "Don't repeat this to anyone, please, but the doggy-doo he's been finding doesn't match any DNA we have on record."

"Somebody has a secret dog?" I asked.

"Looks that way." He pointed to the kitchen. "Would you like some French toast? I have two pieces waiting to cook for you, then I have to go to work."

"Sure it's not too much trouble?"

"Not at all." As he tossed the decadent concoction around

in his frying pan, he told me how to get home. "Look for the yellow house with the hideous green statues, that's your reference point."

"Okay," I agreed. I stuffed my face the moment the toast hit the plate, and I watched him loading the dishwasher.

He got dressed as I rinsed my dish and added it to the load already in the machine.

"You want to hang out here awhile?" he asked me.

"No . . . I think I'll go home and take a shower. What should I do with the sheets?"

"Leave them. I'll take care of them later."

We walked down the street together. We admired the trees, plants, exotic flowers, some of which I'd never seen before, and then I saw the yellow house. He was right about the hideous green statues. How had I not noticed them before?

I stared at the, er, anatomically correct pubes. "My God," I said. "There are actual jewels and um . . . hairs on them."

"Yeah. Some people will do anything to attract attention." Zeca pointed to the stairs. "Happy trails!"

"Thanks, cuz."

He took off for the café, and I climbed Mount Rushmore. I counted hundreds of steps, but it might have been closer to a hundred. I was wheezing by the time I reached the top. I was sweating and there on the path right under my shoe was . . .

A great big pile of dogshit.

Oh, swell. I looked around. No dogs or creeping-away owners in sight. I removed my shoe and let myself into Toppy's house. I walked out the back door to the garden and found the hose. I love the intricate patterns on the soles of state-of-the-art running shoes. Until I have to wedge dogshit out of them.

In the bathroom, I threw the shoes into the washing machine with a few of my clothes. I made and drank coffee whilst I waited, standing in the kitchen with the back door open. I leaned against the doorframe, staring at the gorgeous backyards around me.

The washing machine finished. I could tell because the insane pounding sound had stopped. I put my coffee cup in the sink, walked inside to take my stuff out of the washer, and returned to find Toppy's half-clad statuesque girlfriend in the kitchen.

She pumped up her breasts that were already spilling out of the top of her dress.

"Buongiorno," she said in a breathless way that frightened me.

Boy was she barking up the wrong tree . . .

"What's going on?" a voice asked. Toppy loomed behind her.

"Nothing. I'm just trying to hang my laundry on the line!"

"What's that smell?" He sniffed.

Smell? Was it Angelina's perfume?

"It's your shoes." Toppy wrinkled his nose. "They smell like dog shit."

"I just washed them."

"Wash them again and use the hot cycle." He opened the broom closet and handed me a box of detergent that had his smiling face on it. Angelina giggled when Toppy dragged her out of the house again.

I returned to the bathroom, washed everything once more and this time even I could smell the difference. I took a quick shower and got dressed, then hung the wet things on the line. I couldn't remember the last time I'd line-dried anything and realized how much I missed the smell of the sun on my sheets and clothes.

I checked the time. A little after noon. I should really call my parents. I flopped onto Toppy's living room sofa. The place was quiet, and I wouldn't have minded doing absolutely fuck-all, but I'd promised to work. I had no excuses, so I called my mother's cell phone. I got her voice mail. I felt relieved, actually. I let her know I was in Italy, that things had gone haywire in Greece but that I was okay. I told her I'd stay in touch and that she could always call or text me. I'd just finished up the call when Toppy walked through the back door again.

"You heading down to the caf?" he asked. I loved how he pronounced it the British way, caf.

"Yep."

"Listen, I gotta ask you. Did you see Angie putting anything in the food or drink in the kitchen?" He seemed nervous.

"No. She was just standing there. Why?"

He chewed at his top lip. I'd forgotten that endearing little habit of his.

"She's into spells and stuff. I found a jar of nails buried in the back garden once, and she filed her fingernails into my coffee."

"Are you kidding me?"

He shook his head. "It's a kind of country magic . . . *magia nera*. Black magic."

"She told you this?"

"No. I hear her talking sometimes. She and her friends. They all do this."

"And you're . . . still with her?"

He lifted his hands. "The sex is unreal. Crazy chicks are the hottest." He grabbed my arm. "But do me a favor, be on the lookout."

"Sure," I said, vowing myself to never eat anything in this house.

"I got you the number of an attorney," Toppy said. "He's in Rome, but I figure you can email him and get the ball rolling. He's supposed to be a really great guy." He took his wallet out of his back pocket, extracted a piece of paper and gave it to me. I thanked him and left the house.

Outside, somebody had cleaned up the dog poop I'd stepped in. I walked down the stairs and made a right. I spotted an elderly woman with the world's most ancient, decrepit-looking dog. The dog almost keeled over in an effort to poop, and I noticed the woman almost fell picking it up with a plastic bag.

She smiled at me, and they both went on their rickety way. *Dang.* Now Antonio had me on the poopy prowl . . .

I walked over toward Café Toppy and saw that Zeca was slammed. I'd hoped to just stroll a bit, but he seemed so pleased to see me and for the extra help that I couldn't say no. I went into the kitchen where even Josep and Alen were happy to see me.

"You survived Angie's curse," Josep said, smiling at me.

"Say what?"

His eyes widened. "Er . . . nothing. A small joke. Can you take these frittatas over to table nine?"

"Sure." I gave him a confident smile and felt a bit like Manuel, the hopelessly inadequate waiter from *Fawlty Towers*, trying to find table nine.

"That one over there," Zeca said, rushing off to make coffee. I was a bit staggered, frankly, to see that table nine contained Crisanto and a handsome, light-skinned black man I was sure I'd seen around the hotel pool the day before.

"Thanks," Crisanto said, without any trace of recognition. "Any sign of the coffees we ordered?"

"Just coming up, sir. Enjoy your meals."

I went behind the counter where Zeca had evidently been watching me. "Those guys turned up super late for breakfast. The only reason I served them food was because he's your friend, but he has been an ass since the moment he got here."

"Sorry."

"Did you reject him?"

"Um . . . yeah. A little."

"Ah, that explains it. His feelings are hurt. Here, take the coffees to him." He slid two perfect cappuccinos toward me and wiggled his brow. "But obviously he couldn't stay away. You want a coffee, heartbreaker?"

"I'd love it, thanks." I did feel nervous going back to table nine, perched in the shade just outside the door. Crisanto might have been behaving very badly, but he was still hot. Today he wore red track pants, red and white track shoes, a sleeveless white tank top, and what looked like a vintage pork pie hat.

He tried so hard to act nonchalant, but he smiled when I brought him his coffee.

"Any sign of the toast?" he asked. Oops. I was wrong. He wasn't smiling. He was like a damned crocodile waiting to bite.

"Let me check for you . . . sir." Two could play at the I-don't-know-you game.

In the kitchen, Josep pounced on me. He thrust two plates containing hunks of rustic bread into my hands. "The one on the left is the organic wheat and flaxseed for the Brazilian superstar out there. You can tell that rude shit he has a long way to go before he's Pelé."

"Er . . . okay." I took the plates outside. I was relieved to know that I wasn't the only one on the receiving end of Crisanto's ire.

"Are they still warm?" he griped when I handed him his plate. I smiled at him. I was thinking about Josep's comments. I would never, ever be rude to one of Toppy's guests, but I did like the idea of cutting Crisanto down a peg or two by repeating the crack about Pelé. But I couldn't. Pelé was the Brazilian superstar, probably the greatest soccer player of all time, and I suspected Crisanto was pretty damned great, too.

"If it isn't, sir, I'm happy to bring you more." I waited. Crisanto looked up at me. Evidently, my polite response annoyed him.

"You don't need to hover. If we need something, we'll let you know."

His friend laughed.

That did it. I was a nice person but no pushover. "I find it very hard to believe that anyone would ever cloak you to death!" I said. I turned on my heel and stalked into the kitchen.

I heard Zeca following me and thought I was about to get fired.

"Cloaked to death?" he asked. He laughed so hard that I felt I had to explain it. Josep and Alen also wanted to know what was going on, but then Crisanto showed up at the door. We all stopped talking. His gaze met mine. He put his hands on his hips. He looked down. Had he been on a soccer field, I would have sworn he was sizing up a goal kick. The weight of the world seemed to be on his shoulders.

"Can I talk to you?" he asked.

"Sure." My legs wouldn't move of their own accord. I'd walked away from this guy, and he was about to suck me back in. I was like Al Pacino in *The Godfather* except I had no script in hand. I'd have to fumble for my own words.

Zeca gave me a little push, and I stumbled forward. Crisanto and I walked out into the sun. His breakfast companion had gone.

"I'm sorry," he said. "I . . . I came here to see you, and you weren't here. Henry was the one who made me come. He's been with me here for the last two hours. I got angry because I thought you were with some other guy."

His confession made me smile. *He really thought I was with some other guy?*

"Why are you smiling? This is a shitty thing. I don't want to care about you."

"I don't want to care about you either." Boy was I a liar, liar pants on fire.

"What time do you finish your shift?"

My brain had officially stopped functioning. I was staring at his mouth, and I wanted to kiss him.

He stared at me. I blinked. Nothing came to my head.

"Five o'clock," a little voice whispered from my thigh. I looked down. It was Josep, crouched down, gathering dirty plates from the table beside Crisanto's.

"Five o'clock," I repeated.

"Can I see you then?"

I nodded. Now my heart was racing, and I knew I was gonna screw up all the lunch orders, but I didn't care.

"Thank you," Crisanto said. He seemed really happy then. He touched my hand briefly, and his friend came back out to us. Crisanto introduced us.

"Henry, this is Marius."

We shook hands. "I've heard about nothing else all day," Henry said. He was very handsome. He had a British accent, and suddenly, I realized he was an actor. He had a hit vampire series on TV.

"I'm a big fan of yours," I said. Henry laughed. "I've been hearing all about your mutant triplets."

Oh, sheesh . . .

I grinned. "Well, they're not bad kids really. They're just misunderstood." The three of us laughed. I had to get back to work. I returned to the kitchen, where I helped Alen and Josep prepare the lunch.

We were a better team this afternoon, and I found I wasn't so intimidated by the crush of people. At some point, Crisanto and Henry took off but left me a very generous tip.

The afternoon flew by, and when Crisanto returned alone just before five, it was the first time all day that I almost dropped something.

Zeca and Alex arrived to help me close up. They insisted we all toast each other with limoncello.

Josep was warming up to me a little. Alen seemed as shy . . . or as reticent as ever.

I learned the two friends—Josep said they were not a couple—had backpacked through Europe together and had fallen in love with Italy.

"We have a place in Roma," he said, pronouncing it the Italian way, "but we came here to eat last summer, and Toppy offered us work. We love it here. I hope to come back every summer!"

He told me that he and Alen wanted to open a restaurant on the water in a yacht. "We'll offer a tasting menu and the best Italian wines."

"That sounds great," I said.

We began to clean the floors and close up. Even Crisanto locked a few of the accordion doors. "Can I steal him away now?" he asked Alex at five-forty-five.

"Sure." Zeca grinned at him. He gave me a hug, whispering, "Great job today," in my ear and we left the café.

"Why are you working here?" Crisanto asked me as we walked away.

"My uncle asked me to help." Actually, I'd been staggered by the amount of tips I'd received. I could live very well in Capri on those alone.

We started climbing the stairs to Toppy's house. "I told you last night I'd had some trouble in Athens."

"Right, I remember. Where are we going?"

"My uncle's house."

He quirked a brow at me. "And we are doing this because?"

"I'm tired, and I need a shower."

"We could have one at the hotel . . . have a nice swim."

I nodded. "I still need to change and get my swimsuit."

"Okay," he agreed.

We got to the top and, as usual, I was on the verge of a cardiac arrest, but he hadn't even broken a sweat.

As we got to the house, I felt suddenly shy being alone with him. He followed me inside, and I turned around.

"Can I get you something to drink?" I remembered Angie's weirdness and almost recanted the offer, but he was all over me then. He pressed me against the closed door, his mouth on mine. I made sure the door was locked, but I was still trying to breathe properly, and he wasn't helping me.

"We're alone, right?" he asked.

"I don't know."

He took a step back. I could see his cock was hard, wedged right across the front of his running pants. Oh, boy. He was huge.

"Where's your room?"

I pointed upstairs. My mind almost broke down at the prospect of more climbing, but we made it, and we could see we were alone. I showed him the way to my room, and he smiled as he looked around.

"You mentioned a shower," he said.

"So I did."

"Go and take one, I'll be here waiting for you." He threw himself on my bed. He must have been raised with the same superstitions I was because he removed his hat and put it on the chair beside the bed.

"Don't come back with clothes on," he commanded.

Oh, God.

I stripped off, and he watched me through half closed eyes. He saw my cock bouncing for joy thanks to him. His smile widened.

"You need to come here with that," he said, his voice low. "I don't think it can wait for you to shower."

I swallowed. Hard. I closed the door and inched back toward him. He kept beckoning me with the crook of his right index finger until I was up close and personal with his mouth. He used his finger to catch hold of my cock. He placed a light kiss on the head.

"Pleased to meet you, beautiful."

I hardened even more, and the guy had hardly touched me.

He dropped my cock and gazed up at me, raising his mouth for a kiss. I gave him one. He pulled me down on the bed beside him, his kisses turning deep and fierce. His hands roamed my body but didn't touch my cock. I let him be in control. To be honest, my cock was ready to explode just from his kisses . . . not that this had never happened to me before.

He kept kissing me, then placed me on my back. He touched and kissed my nipples. Squeezed them. He sucked them, which was a huge turn-on. His hand raked down my chest and belly, skipped my cock and moved underneath me. He held my balls in his hand as if testing their measure.

I felt his index finger working the base of my ball sac as he massaged my balls. His finger moved down, touching my perineum and he seemed to know exactly where to press. I stifled a groan.

He moved me to my side. He began licking me from the base of my neck across my shoulder, down my arm, occasionally stopping to suck at me. He discovered places that turned me on that I'd never known to be hot spots for me, such as the back of my elbow. I felt drunk with passion. Outside my windows, which were open to the breeze, olive and lemon trees swayed with the breeze.

Crisanto's tongue rolled up to my shoulder blade, and I

shivered as it moved back down to the slight curve of my hip. He licked down my thigh, then spoke.

"Lift your leg," he commanded.

I did as I was told. He didn't wait. His mouth engulfed my asshole the second he saw it. He licked and sucked at me, and fire began to ignite deep within my belly. I longed to touch myself, but he must have sensed this because he moved my hand away.

Holding my breath, I let the emotions, the incredible sensations wash over me. Like a tidal wave, I began to come. I had never come from a man just licking my ass before, and I was surprised how deep and intense it was. Rivulets of pain from a headache I'd had for two days and ignored seared down the back of my neck, stuttering at my tail bone and vanished.

Crisanto licked and sucked until he thought I'd had enough. I couldn't speak, couldn't move . . . and then he rolled me onto my back, to examine my still-hard cock.

"You needed that," he said and began to lick my belly.

CHAPTER FIVE

He didn't do much more than taste me, then he sent me to shower. I was a little shocked to return to him having gone through my suitcase and selecting the things he wanted me to wear.

"This swimsuit is no good," he said, holding up my black swim trunks.

"What's wrong with it?"

"It's . . . old man's panties!"

"No. It's Galliano!"

"Old man's panties. At the hotel, I will give you the perfect swimsuit for you to wear." He cupped my balls in his hand. "Get dressed."

"Yes, sir!"

He grinned. "You might regret saying that."

"I'm sure I will." I threw on the clothes he'd picked out, slipping my feet into the flip-flops he insisted I wear. I had the bizarre feeling that I was playing hooky and yet I knew I wasn't. I'd finished my workday such as it was . . . and now it seemed I was waiter-putty in Crisanto's hands.

When we left the house and walked to the hotel, he started asking questions about Athens. Serious questions about the Greek real estate agent and the attorney. I told him that Uncle Toppy had given me an attorney's name and he immediately wanted to know who it was. He didn't walk close beside me. We might have just been a couple of swells, as my dad would say, walking down the street. It was not until he key-carded the hotel's gate that he came anywhere near me.

As we walked up the lavender flower-lined path, he put his hand on my ass. Inside the hotel, Hugh and Alex were running around as usual. Somehow, they managed to make it look easy as if the job weren't stressful. Maybe to them, it wasn't.

"Did you—" Crisanto started to ask.

"In your room." Alex gave me a wink. We walked upstairs, and Crisanto unlocked the door to his private paradise.

"Take off those fucking clothes," he instructed, his mouth meeting mine.

I didn't need written instructions. He moved away from me, closed the door and returned, throwing off my clothes. He pushed me into a chair, thrusting my legs over the sides. Hot damn. His tongue was back in my ass, but this time he worked his magic over my cock and balls. He licked me, slowly, driving me crazy.

When he finally took my cock into his mouth, I thought I would come, but he gripped the base and worked me. He tugged on me, hard, taking me into his mouth all the way, then forcing me out again. He sucked the head back in, and finally, I couldn't take anymore.

"Uh-huh," he murmured around my cock as his mouth tightened and he plunged back down again.

He worked a finger into my ass. It surprised me how much I wanted it. I hadn't bottomed much . . . but I had a feeling that was soon about to change.

I came hard, Crisanto staying on me. He kept sucking as my eruption seemed to never want to end. He was something else.

When he finally released me, he rejected the idea of my reciprocating.

"Later. I want to show you off by the pool." He stood and

walked over to the coffee table, where he held up two tiny matching black swimsuits. I was incredulous.

"They won't cover anything," I said.

"They will cover enough," he retorted. "Dinner in our room tonight?"

I was still sprawled in the chair. I wasn't just putty, I was like a brie left out to warm to room temperature, and I'd spread myself all over the plate.

How had I gone from being the brave, smart man who walked away from him to practically begging for him to let me suck his cock?

He tugged my hand and brought me to my feet. "Put this on."

He handed me one of the tiny bikinis, and I have to say I felt damned sexy in it. When he ran a hand across my cock and got me all hot and bothered again, I could tell he was pleased.

He moved away from me and dropped his tracksuit pants.

Commando . . . oh man, I loved a man who went commando . . .

His cock was uncut, and I instantly coveted it.

"Please . . . I gotta touch you."

"Patience," he said, but I could tell he was pleased. He slid his swimsuit up his legs and up his thighs, and I couldn't wait to come back and remove that thing with my teeth. He had an unbelievable body.

He grabbed his wallets, key card, and a couple of towels.

"Ready?" he asked. We left the room, and as we walked out to the pool, I noticed several couples in matching swimsuits. Crisanto was letting people know I was his . . . but also that he was mine.

As we staked out a pair of chaises by the pool, Hugh came over to us.

"Can I bring you something to drink?"

Crisanto looked at me. "What would you like, sweet man?"

"Campari and soda," I said. It was one of my favorite cocktails, and it seemed perfect in my over-heated state.

"That sounds good. I'd like one too, please."

Hugh nodded and left us alone. We dropped our things on the chaises and made our way to the pool. It felt amazing to submerge myself in the cool water. The temperature was perfect, the sun glinting off the small ripples. To re-emerge into his waiting arms was like a porn movie come to life.

He kissed me as we danced around in the water. Then he pushed himself back from me and began to splash me. A couple of guys got into the pool and joined in. A few complained about the noise and the splashing, but soon we were all playing Marco Polo. I couldn't remember the last time I'd played it.

I discovered something about both of us within minutes. We both cheat at Marco Polo. He was supposed to be looking for us, eyes closed of course, but he was fully looking underwater. When I caught him, he laughed, swallowing a lot of water. He caught me next, then it was my turn. He caught me looking, too.

"You two are possibly the worst Marco Polo players I've ever met," Hugh said when we came out of the pool, leaving the others to it.

"We have room for improvement, certainly," Crisanto said.

We exchanged glances and burst out laughing. Hugh helped us get settled, handed us each tall, frosted glasses with our Campari and offered us sample bites of the evening's appetizers, currently under construction in the kitchen.

"This is our new arancini, deep-fried ricotta balls. We are serving them tonight two ways; with homemade marinara or black volcanic salt salsa. Might I suggest dipping it into both sauces?"

He beamed at us then left us to scarf down the arancini. The ricotta exploded in my mouth. The warm, runny cheese held a hint of oregano, nutmeg, and . . . something else. I licked my fingers. I wanted more, but all of a sudden Alex was by our side, his face ashen.

"Marius, we've had another robbery."

I looked at him. Why was he telling me this? He was gesturing with his head, but I was hardly dressed for sleuthing work. Crisanto was staring at me.

"Er . . . I'll be back," I said. I blew him a kiss and went off with my cousin.

"Thank you," Alex said, looking relieved. "Some of the guests think you are our new security guy."

"Why do they think that?" I hurried to keep up with Alex.

"They saw you with Antonio. And let's not forget you played a private investigator for twelve years."

"That's ridiculous. I'm an actor."

"Yeah . . . well . . . Antonio's on his way. I'm just freaked the hell out, and you're so great with people." He paused. "Actually, the victim's a big fan of yours. He asked me where the mutant triplets were."

"Oh?"

"Yeah. I told them they were in a sanatorium in Vienna."

"You . . . what?"

"Brilliant, wasn't it? Anyway, poor Antonio was here all day, and he had to go . . ." He looked at me, his face crumpled with sudden grief. "One of the stores in town got hit."

"Hit?"

"Robbed." His voice dropped.

"You're kidding." I couldn't compute this. "That has to be the first time in . . . how many years?"

"Seventeen."

I gaped at him.

"I know, right?" He led me to his office and shut the door. He looked me up and down. "Here." He opened the door to a closet that cleverly looked like part of a wall. He pulled out a shirt and a pair of pants.

"You won't need a tie. What size shoes do you wear?"

"Nine."

"These loafers will fit."

"Why am I doing this?"

"To help me. Just be nice until Antonio gets here. He'll be back as soon as he can." He looked so bleak I reached across and hugged him and took the clothes out of his hand. "It's more of a PR exercise than anything else." He let out a ragged sigh. "People saw you with Antonio here yesterday, and they think you are consulting with him."

"Consulting with him?"

Alex gave me a brief, tortured smile. "You do exude an aura, you know. I know it's star quality. Dad always says that about you. To the hotel guests, it's an aura of confidence."

"Really?" All of this was news to me, but I loved my family and would do anything to help them.

"The security guy Antonio suggested can't be here until the end of the week and we honestly weren't expecting a robbery. Antonio just said to wing it." He dropped his voice. "And he said not to touch anything with your bare hands. He's bringing a dusting kit here."

"I'm an actor." I pulled on the trousers. "I'll wing it. What happened exactly?"

"Same thing that happened to Crisanto. Got a funny phone call about tapas on the terrace. He went up there and came back to find his laptop gone. The guy is understandably furious."

I thought for a moment. "It's an inside job for sure but . . .

don't you have security cameras?"

"Not yet. We haven't needed them. Antonio ordered some from a security firm in Naples." He looked at me. "Please don't tell anybody. We're going to hide them around the hotel. These are special cameras you embed in objects, sort of like nanny cams."

"I think it's an excellent idea." I picked up a notebook on his desk. He handed me a pen.

As we walked down the hall, he seemed so tense and frightened I didn't know what to say to comfort him. I was surprised to see the guest who'd been robbed was Henry, Crisanto's friend.

"My," he said, looking ridiculously pleased to see me. "I told Crisanto your work at the restaurant had to be a cover." He leaned closer and whispered, "I think it's very cool that you are working so quietly as a security officer." He glanced at me. "Too quietly as it happens." He waved a hand toward the desk in his room.

At first glance, his room seemed smaller, less . . . luxurious than Crisanto's, but I realized he had selected one with a working office. It was like media central with a fax machine, photocopier, and two telephones.

"I'm going to record this on my cell phone as well as make notes if that's all right," I said.

He nodded. "Fine. Whatever."

I turned on the mike function on my cell phone and put it on the bed.

"Please tell me what happened," I said. The less I got into my 'status' here, the better, I thought.

"Well . . ." He scratched his head. "I got a phone call from a guy who . . ." He looked embarrassed for a moment. "He said he'd seen me and thought I was hot. He asked me to come up to the terrace for tapas and maybe more. Unlike my friend Crisanto, I've been rather unlucky since I got here."

Now it was my turn to blush. "Go on."

"Well, I went up there. The guy had a cute voice. Nice accent."

"What kind of accent?"

He spread his hands. "I don't even know what I'd call it . . . kinda . . . European I suppose."

That didn't tell me much.

I saw the space where the laptop had been, and I took a photo with my cell phone's camera.

"Was the door open when you returned?" I asked him.

"Yeah, how did you know?"

"How much was it open?"

"Just ajar." He moved toward the door to show me. "I know I closed and locked it."

I noticed he had jewelry out, a couple of chains, a watch.

"Was any jewelry taken?"

No. I figured they took the laptop because it might be easier to fence."

"Not on Capri," Alex said. "There isn't even an Internet café here, let alone any place they can sell it."

I had an idea. "Does your laptop have Lojack on it?"

"Oh . . . my God. Yes, it does. I didn't even think of that!"

"What's your account number?"

He seemed agitated. "Why didn't I think of it before?" He rifled through his cell phone. "I hate this thing. I use my laptop for everything. I have a book on there I'm halfway through writing. I—here it is. Holy crap, it's searching for it now. How about that? One button and I can—what's this here?"

Henry turned the cell phone around for Alex to view the screen. He looked at me. "Laundry chute."

"Where is it?" I asked. Alex sprinted down the hall. I was right behind him. Alex and I were skinnier than Henry, and we took turns leaning way down into the metal tubing to peer into the chute.

"I don't see it," Alex said.

"Show me the laundry room," I instructed, "and bring me some rubber gloves."

I was relieved that whoever had stolen the laptop had dumped it down the laundry chute, but I knew this had to be a staff job because the chute was well disguised. It blended in with the wall, much like the closet in Alex and Hugh's office.

"Man, I didn't know that was there." Henry scratched his chin. "Fuck, I am so glad my laptop didn't wind up in the washing machine!"

Alex and I sprinted downstairs. Alex found me some gloves, and I pawed through a mountain of dirty linens and towels.

"It's here," I said. "Where do the linens go to be washed?"

He pointed to a dark hallway. "We have industrial grade washers and dryers. I can't believe you found it."

"We'll have to bag it for Antonio to fingerprint," I warned. "Henry won't be happy, but at least we got it back."

"If you hadn't thought of Lojack, this would have been a disaster."

"Antonio would have thought of it." I carried the machine upstairs where Henry looked overjoyed to see his laptop.

"Looks okay," he said running his gaze over it.

"I can't let you have it until we dust it for fingerprints, but I'm pretty certain I can return it to you then. Is that okay?"

"Yeah. Whatever. I'm just so pleased. But I have no idea what the hell to do with myself until then. I came here to write."

"Use a notebook," I said. "Relax by the pool."

"Frustrated writer, are you?"

"Very." I grinned at him.

"I might do that. Where can I get a drink around here?"

"Why don't you sit by the pool, I'll bring you whatever you want ... and may I book you a massage, with our compliments?"

"Yeah ... you may." Henry nodded approvingly. He looked over at me. "I don't suppose you also moonlight as a massage therapist, do you?"

"Sorry, no." I looked at him. "Can I ask you a question?"

"Sure."

"Did you back up your book?"

He winced. "Yeah ... but I've been having trouble with my USB port. I mentioned it to my agent this morning. Why do you ask?"

"Just wondering."

He grinned. "No problem. I wonder where Crisanto's at?" He pulled out his cell phone and took off down the hallway, phone to his ear.

"Let's get this to your office," I said. "We need to talk."

Inside, I told Alex that somebody on his staff had skeleton key cards and was picking people that they knew had certain possessions they deemed important.

"Which of your employees has had direct dealings with both men?" I asked. "These incidents aren't random. I'm positive of that."

"I don't honestly know. As far as the key cards ... there are enough for the room maids, Hugh and I. None of the therapists have key cards." His face turned white. "God ... the idea that one of them could be behind this ..."

"Do those skeleton keys work on this door?"

He shook his head. "No. Hugh and I have special keys that can't be duplicated. We have the hotel safe here for guests' special needs."

"That's good, so I can confidently keep the laptop here until Antonio gets here?"

"Yes, absolutely." His shoulders sagged a little. "This

makes three close calls. Five minutes later and those sheets would have been in the wash."

"Whoever took this must have known that."

"This is the time we wash . . . we wash twice a day, but we offer our guests extra-late checkout, and we also wash in the morning."

I had to tell him my thoughts. "Whoever did this has plants in your rooms."

"No . . . get outta here. That's impossible!"

"Listen, Henry's been having trouble backing up his book. He just said so. He told somebody, and that conversation has been overheard. That or he and Crisanto interacted with the perpetrator in some way. Which of your staff would they have spoken to?"

He whipped open his laptop. "They both call room service a lot. They both ask for a lot of towels." He lifted his shoulders. "It could have been any one of my staff, but I can vouch for them. Antonio checked them all out for me."

"Okay, is there anyone new here?"

"No. I—" He blinked. "Wait. Fuck. But no. It's impossible."

"Who?" I asked.

He looked upset now. "Shit. If it's them, then I'm screwed, Marius. I mean . . . screwed."

There was a knock at the door that startled us both. Alex opened the door to Antonio, who looked exhausted.

He came inside and sat down, thanking me for helping out.

We wanted to know about the store robbery, but he wanted to know about the hotel room theft. We told him quickly.

"Marius thinks it might be the new staff members," Alex said.

Antonio frowned. "What new staff members?"

"You're going to kill me."

"Probably, but I want to hear about it anyway."

"Jesus." Alex covered his face with his hands. "I . . .Hugh . . .I—"

"Out with it, man," I said.

"Yeah. Out with it." Antonio sat up in his chair, arms folded across his chest as if to brace himself for the bad news.

"We have the client in the penthouse suite. I mentioned him to you. He wanted private butlers. But then he wanted round-the-clock staff, so we've put on two extra people. I didn't check 'em out because they work for Dad."

"Are you talking about Josep and Alen?" Antonio gaped at him.

"Yeah." Alex looked helpless. "I thought they'd be okay."

"How long have they been working here?" Antonio asked.

"A couple of days." Alex's face turned ashen. "Just before all this . . . started."

For several, long minutes, Antonio paced the office, Alex and I waiting for his pearls of wisdom.

"We have no proof they're involved, but for now, I suggest you tell Josep and Alen their services are no longer required."

Alex looked miserable. "I need staff." He looked at me. "Are you willing to work up there?"

"Me? But I'm no cook. I'm no butler, either."

He nodded. "You're right. I'll have to come up with somebody else."

Antonio let out a ragged sigh. "I blame myself for this. I never checked out Alen and Josep, even for Toppy, against my better judgment. He vouched for them as sweet, Eastern European guys who needed work. Until I run fingerprints on them, I won't haul them in for questioning. For now, this all remains between the three of us. Okay?"

We all nodded.

He dusted the laptop, said he could find a lot of prints but would run them through his system. "I must get the owner's prints," he muttered.

He then called one of his few staff members and sent the guy to Toppy's Café to dust for fingerprints in the kitchen for comparison. Josep and Alen would have their prints on everything there.

"I think they're up there now with my guest . . . when do I tell him . . . and them?" Alex asked.

"Are they the ones who stay all night?"

"Part of the night. I have three rotating teams of two who work eight-hour shifts."

"Can the two remaining crews work twelve-hour shifts until we find a replacement pair?" Antonio asked.

"Well, yes, but it'll be awfully hard on them. Our client is the most difficult man I've ever met. I want to kill myself after spending five minutes with him. He's horrible." Alex dropped his head on his desk and wept.

My pour cousin. I felt awful for him. I put my arm around him.

"I'm a wreck!" he sobbed. "My whole life I was a fuck-up. I finally settle down, get my act together and —"

"You're doing great," Antonio said, as he bagged everything up. "I would prefer to keep the laptop as evidence, but I've taken plenty of prints and returning it to the owner will restore some good relations between you. Where is he, Alex?" He got up to follow him and turned to me.

"Can you wait here, Marius? I'd like a word with you."

"Sure, I'll wait." I sat there feeling miserable. In one respect it was good . . . I'd done well helping Alex, and we had a lead on two suspects.

On the other hand was the question of whether Crisanto and Henry had had any contact with Alen and Josep. Had they all had a swinging party?

Crisanto had told me he didn't want anything serious. Just fun. How much fun had he had with those two?

Quit it, fool. You just met him. He owes you nothing. You're reaching here. You're taking giant leaps . . . there's nothing to say he fooled around with them and mentioned his dual passports—

Alex returned, Hugh in tow.

"Thank you for what you did," Hugh said. He reached down and hugged me. We sat in the office waiting for Antonio. He returned about fifteen minutes later.

"Henry is good friends with the gentleman guest upstairs," Antonio said. "He said the man is a famous designer and that he and Crisanto went up there for drinks. I didn't let on we suspected Josep and Alen. I simply asked if he'd ever been upstairs before and he volunteered the information."

Antonio seemed to relax. "I must say it relieves my mind that we have a promising lead." He looked at me. "I have a question for you."

"Ask away."

"You did an excellent job here today, and I commend you for it. You thought fast, and you handled a delicate situation well. I know this is a little . . . unusual . . . but would you consider spending the next few days acting as the security officer for the hotel?"

"I—"

"If you're worried about Toppy, I'll clear it with him. I need somebody here I trust, and my staff has its hands full right now."

"I don't have any experience doing security work."

"Yes, you do." He grinned at me. "Toppy said you used to be a bouncer and a security guard before you got your acting job."

"Oh, my God. That was twelve years ago!"

"Not much has changed, and I think this should be fairly

routine."

"I was a bouncer at a titty bar. Not the same thing!"

"Good practice though," he insisted. "Up until now, this hotel has run very smoothly. However, if you prefer chopping vegetables and having people scream at you . . ."

"No, no. I'll do it. Do I get to carry a gun?" I was starting to get excited now.

Antonio rolled his eyes. "No, Rambo, you don't. You will be a very unobtrusive but quietly forceful presence."

"That doesn't sound like fun. I want to beat people up."

"Sorry about that." He smirked. "We may already be eliminating the problem here by removing Josep and Alen, but we can't be too careful. You mentioned room bugs earlier, and I think we need to consider it. I'm doing a scan of each room for electronic bugs as each room becomes available. I'll need your help on that. I have a surveillance kit arriving first thing in the morning.

"I'll go over the first room with you, and we can take it from there. I want you here in this office and strolling the grounds in a casual way. You will wear a T-shirt and trousers, relaxed, Capri style. No guns, no Tasers." He stared at me. "No beating up! You and I will stay in touch . . ." He glanced at Alex and back at me. "If there is any sign, the smallest sign of trouble, I expect you to contact me."

He looked worried for a moment. "If Josep and Alen are our troublemakers, then we need to keep an eye on them. If they are not allowed here, then they will focus their efforts on the township."

"Tell us about the store robbery," I said.

Antonio shook his head. "It's a hate crime. Pure and simple. It involves a gay store owner. Understand . . . this is an elderly man in a private relationship . . . very, very discreet, for forty years. He is devastated. He is talking about leaving Capri."

"Are you talking about Signore Brusco?" Alex looked horrified.

Antonio nodded.

"But he's so sweet. He wouldn't harm a fly."

"Which makes the attack especially brutal." Antonio took his cell phone out and scrolled through it. "This is what they did to him."

I was shocked to see the window of a dress shop smashed, and somebody had spray-painted *fags* in red across the window, the clothing, and the floor.

My eyes could not absorb the shock of the nastiness I was seeing. *Fags* painted all over the once beautiful store

"They ransacked the cash register, but there were only about fifty-five Euros in there." He took his cell phone back after we'd all looked at the photos. "It was the principle of the thing. This man's family lost everything during Mussolini's reign. He was a child during that time. To him, he is being victimized all over again."

"This is horrible," I said. "Is there anything we can do to help him?"

Antonio's expression darkened. "We will do everything we can. I brought over glass specialists on a police launch from Naples. They have done an excellent job cleaning up every last shard of glass. Remember this is a walking island . . . people often don't wear shoes. They've boarded up the store. My men have done a wonderful job keeping amateur photographers away. We've kept the entire attack under wraps. There were fingerprints that do not belong to Signore Brusco on the cash register, so we'll compare these to Alen's and Josep's prints."

He lapsed into silence.

"We live in secrecy . . . all of us who are gay here. We live amongst others . . . we love, care for, and join in with everybody else . . . with the sort of shame that is pitiful. Pitiful! It is not our shame, but others' shame, that we must shoulder. I willingly shoulder it because I love my man.

"Signore Brusco is one of the few men on the island who is accepted for the very reason that he is gay and yet . . . he doesn't do any of the things straight people associate with gay culture. He is a refined, wonderful man . . . he's reached out to gay teens over the years. He is a beacon of light for all. Gay, straight, white, black, yellow, pink. That's why this is particularly bad.

"I've had Toppy look after him all day. I think he's calmed down a little, but this was an expensive case of robbery and vandalism. Even with insurance, in Italy these things take time, so he'll have to pay for all the repairs, then claim it on his insurance. Otherwise, he'll spend most of the summer with his store boarded up."

God . . .

"I think we all need to band together . . . all the young gay men on the island . . . anyone actually, and paint and recarpet . . . do whatever we can for him," I said.

Antonio thought this was a great idea. "I'll organize it. The new glass for the window arrives in two days." He looked at me. "See . . . I was wise to ask you for help." He checked his watch. "I have two officers patrolling the streets. Toppy and Zeca will trade places with them at midnight. I am swapping with another officer along the *terrazzina*."

"I want to help," Hugh said.

"So do I," Alex chorused.

"No. You are better off staying here, keep things running smoothly. Marius, get some rest. I want to see you here at nine o'clock tomorrow morning."

"No problem." I left the office with him with a heavy heart. My cell phone started to ring. It was a number I didn't recognize. When I took the call, Antonio held up his hand in farewell and left me to it.

"Marius?" I didn't place the voice at first until the man

said, "I saw you leaving the office. Were you going to run off without saying goodbye?"

I couldn't help smiling. "Crisanto, where are you?"

"Down by the pool, where you left me."

I looked out there and saw him giving me a little finger wave. Henry was sitting beside him. I went out to join them. Crisanto stood and greeted me with a warm kiss. Seconds later, Alex arrived. "Would you like a Campari?" he asked me. "Or can I bring you something else?"

"Campari would be nice, thanks."

"Dinner's going to be just a few minutes." He rushed off again.

"I invited Henry to join us for dinner," Crisanto said. "I know we talked about having dinner in our room."

Our room. For some reason, this tickled me. "No, that's wonderful. Gives me a chance to talk to Henry more about his writing."

Henry liked that, I could tell.

With Crisanto sitting between us, a protective — or was it a possessive — hand on my lap, we talked about writing, movies, acting, and life as we proceeded to demolish one of crustiest, lightest, most flavorful pizzas I'd ever had in my life. When it first arrived, I thought the ricotta filling in the middle of it looked dense and heavy. It was actually a mix of four cheeses, arugula, and a dash of freshly chopped chili. It was sublime. We washed it down with a fresh round of drinks, and then I begged off dessert. I couldn't eat another thing.

Crisanto was brilliant company. He could talk about anything, as could Henry. Crisanto proved to have a delightful sense of humor and always deflected talk of his own accomplishments, which I found refreshing.

"I must confess I Googled you," Henry told me. "I thought I'd seen you somewhere and it was in a werewolf movie, *The Fang*, which I believe was shot in Prague. What was that experience like?"

"Oh," I said. "That was amazing! We shot in an actual Catholic cemetery, and we began to worry that maybe we should ask permission. We went to the Catholic priest, and he frowned . . . he asked us exactly what we'd be doing. The director and I had elected to go and talk to him. He thought . . ." I felt myself blushing. "He thought maybe I could charm him."

"I'm sure you did," Crisanto said.

"Well . . . I don't know how charming I was, but we were honest. We told him there would be fake blood and crucifixes, half-naked virgins and—"

Crisanto and Henry laughed.

"And he listened very closely and finally said, "Excellent. I've been trying to get a bishop here in Prague for years. This'll get me one for sure! Make sure there are buckets of fake blood!"

They loved the story. Henry told me he had a fondness for werewolves and the book he was working on was the retooling of an ancient legend.

"Sounds great," I said.

"Tell me you'll be in the movie version and it will be."

I grinned. "You got it." I couldn't remember when I'd had such fun. I tried not to think about the following morning or the problems on the island. I enjoyed being with Crisanto and Henry. Some invisible moment seemed to pass between them. Henry told us he'd had a wonderful time, hugged us both, and excused himself.

We watched him go over to the bar where a couple of cute guys were drinking frothy-looking drinks with umbrellas poking over the rims. I stood, and Crisanto's ever-present hand moved around my waist as he joined me.

"Would you like to have our coffee upstairs?" His decadent smile held the promise of so much more, but I shook my head.

"I want to . . . believe me I want to, but I can't."

"Can't? Why not?"

I took a deep breath. This was killing me. I was thoroughly enjoying the man's company. He was the hottest thing on two legs . . . and I longed to tangle in his probably four-thousand count bed sheets.

"For the next few days, I'm working here and—"

"That's ridiculous. You're working security, right?"

I nodded.

"You're very safe with me. We're being discreet remember?"

"Not so discreet. We're all over each other," I said with a grin.

"And your cousins and the cop already know about us. Alex was the one who gave me your cell phone number. Did Antonio tell you to stay away from me?"

"No," I admitted.

"Well, I admire your ethics and your fabulous mind and body. Please let me admire them a little more . . . intimately."

"Okay," I said and gulped.

Chapter Six

If I'd had any fantasies that I'd be in for a good, solid, old-fashioned fucking, I couldn't have been more wrong. Crisanto led me back to his room. The promise of coffee apparently forgotten I got something better.

Him.

He pressed me against the wall, peppering my mouth, face, throat, and hands with kisses. I was tickled at how carefully he removed my borrowed clothes and hung them in the closet.

"You'll need them in the morning," he said. "What time must I return you?"

"I need to be downstairs at nine."

"Good. I'll order breakfast for seven." He glanced down at my hardening cock, now wedged painfully inside the tiny black swimsuit.

"Leave those on," he said. He dropped to his knees and sucked the length of my shaft through the fabric. He spun me around, his tongue making lazy eights on my ass. He began to concentrate his efforts on my crack, his tongue digging deeper and deeper. When his finger slid under the leg elastic, and his mouth sought my butt cheek, I moaned, pressing against him. His tongue and finger slid across to the crack. I could tell he had some game plan because after a few licks he released me. He turned me around and kissed me, his own cock hard now inside his tiny swimsuit.

"Come with me," he said.

As if I would go anyplace else . . .

92

He led me into the gigantic bathroom. There was a huge, four-head shower, a spa bath and, right in the middle of the room, a table. Above it hung a long nozzle with an adjustable showerhead that seemed to be the focus of his attention. I'd never seen anything like this setup—except at a day spa my mum took me to once for a mani-pedi and body scrub but—

I could see the firelight in his eyes as he began kissing me again. He pushed me onto the table, which had a springy fabric on it. He began to circle me, his gaze back on me now. As I lay on my back, he leaned into me, kissing me again, his hands roaming my body.

"I've been thinking about this moment since the first second I saw you." He covered my mouth with his before I could ask a question or say something stupid. He moved away from me. I heard him opening drawers and was surprised when he returned with a brown bottle. He uncapped it and poured oil onto his hands. I could smell all kinds of good things. Mint, honey, cinnamon. And oh, boy, he began giving me a rubdown with it. My whole body tingled.

"What is that?" I asked.

"Sex oil from Brazil." My body heat ramped up several notches as he bent and began to suck my cock. He took his mouth away from me.

"Turn over, Marius. Get on your knees."

I did as I was told and he began oiling my back and, mercy, my ass. His tongue and fingers began probing my hole. Feverish heat sent sweat from the top of my head into my eyes and down my back.

With two fingers in me now, he moved around, pulled my face toward him and kissed me, giving me lots of tongue.

"I'm going to blindfold you now."

He produced a black eye mask that he slipped over my

eyes. I became more aware of the heat through my body, my racing heartbeat, and his insistent fingers at my ass. I gasped when he moved away again.

"Don't go," I begged.

He soon returned without a word and dropped a kiss on my lips. He must have known I needed more because he moved away, then returned. Suddenly, I felt something at my ass.

"What the hell is that?" I asked. It felt soft, yet rigid. Bigger than any sex toy I'd ever fooled around with. "I feel fingers," I said. He worked the toy into me. I tried to reach around to feel. My God. When he let me touch it I realized it was a kind of artificial hand, the fingers meeting into a point. He resumed stroking my ass, alternating with the hand and his tongue, then letting me have the fingers. That thing was working its way into me, my first experience of being almost fisted, and I was surprised how much I liked it.

My cock was ready to explode. He backed off after giving me a few short cock-strokes.

Damn.

He moved away again and returned, this time with a vibrator. I'd never had one in my mouth or ass, but he gave it to me to suck.

"Ready for a threesome?" he asked, as I tried valiantly taking the huge toy into my mouth. He kissed my face as I sucked and then, he turned around and started working it into my ass. My head hit the table as soon as I felt the vibrations go through me. *God help me* . . . it wasn't even in me yet, and I was going to come.

I did, with Crisanto's toy burrowing into me, his hand beneath me stroking my cock.

"That's it, Marius," he said, his tone encouraging.

He didn't let up. He kept the toy in me.

"Want to come again?" he asked. I knew he wanted me to say yes.

"Yes."

"Turn over."

He kept the vibrator in me. "Fuck my cock," he said, his mouth descending to my belly and cock. He licked up my juices. I couldn't stand it anymore. I reached for him. His cock was so hard, it poked over the top of his swimsuit.

The vibrator inside me started moving faster, then annoyingly slow. He wanted me to beg for it, and I did as I finally, finally got my mouth on his gargantuan cock. His uncut shaft tasted like salt and honey. I held onto him by grabbing his balls. He hissed. I couldn't see but was pretty sure he liked it. He abruptly took it away from me.

"I love that you are still so hard, Marius." He was working up more heat inside my ass. A little more of the toy dug into me. God . . . it was against my prostate now and the sensations were fucking amazing. My legs began to shake.

"Suck me, baby," he said, and I moved my mouth back onto him. He was close to coming and so, unbelievably, was I. He reached up for the nozzle and warm water began to fall on me, on us . . . warm rain, with a hard cock in my ass and a delicious one in my mouth.

My orgasm was so intense it shuddered through me, red and purple flames and sparks of gold fusing in my brain. He lost all control then, coming himself. His cock went deep into my throat as he gave me everything he had. The vibrator inside my ass didn't stop until he turned off the water and withdrew the toy from me.

I lay on the table shaking. We were drenched, but far from spent. He picked me up and carried me to the bed in his room. With the doors open, the cool breeze was welcoming.

"How about some coffee, some soufflé, and then I'll fuck you until you can't take any more?" he asked.

"Yes, please."

I was walking funny, very funny, by the time I showed up at the office in the morning. I had so many hickeys on my ass and crotch I didn't think I would be able to wear anything less than old-fashioned swimming knickers for the next two weeks . . . not that I cared. Crisanto was the most inventive, ardent lover I'd ever had. He'd awoken me with kisses and a mind-blowing rim job.

He had a vicious streak running through him, though, because he made me go for a run with him at dawn. Now I could barely move.

Antonio was waiting for me as I hobbled into the office. Man, I hurt so good . . .

He looked a lot less happy than I did.

"How was everything last night?" I asked. "No more trouble?"

"No. I just had a police launch here with five more officers from Naples. I know two of them and don't trust them at all, but I will send them back with Josep and Alan if they turn out to be the culprits.

"And at least we'll have three new recruits who can stroll the promenade . . . make our people feel safe, and let the bad guys know we're watching them."

Alex joined us. "I did as you asked, and my guest wasn't happy, but he understood about replacing Josep and Alen. He told Hugh he'd been thinking about investing in their yacht restaurant."

"God," Antonio said. "What about Josep and Alen?"

"I told them they are not to contact him privately. I believe them when they say they won't. Both parties have had to go through Hugh up until now to make contact, and he won't pass out phone numbers."

"Good," Antonio said.

"How long do we have to wait to find out if it's Josep and

Alen?" Poor Alex looked like he hadn't slept a wink.

"Don't worry. I'm waiting for the fingerprint analysis this morning. We should know within the hour if we have a hit. If we do, one of my own officers and I will be escorting them off the island. I have the police launch waiting."

He held up a kit. "The officers brought the kit I ordered. How many rooms are available to search?"

"Three."

"Let's go." We followed Alex to the first room, where he began to assemble his bug detector.

"Oh," I said, smiling with recognition. "It's a SuperBroom."

"You've worked with one before?" Antonio looked ecstatic.

"Only on TV."

"Good enough." Something pinged in the room, and all three of us stiffened.

"It's in the phone," he said. He held the broom closer to the phone and frowned. "Hold this for me." He handed me the responder. I knew from the little I'd worked with the SuperBroom that it picked up all kinds of things.

"This is weird," he said. "Somebody has put a re-router on the phone."

"What does that mean?" Alex asked.

"It means that when people try to use this phone to call anybody, even the front desk, they won't get there."

"Where do they go?"

"I don't know. Let's see." He put the phone on loud-speaker and dialed O for the hotel operator. Instead, it went to some porn line.

"Well," he said. "How long has this room been vacant?"

"Since yesterday afternoon." Alex's cell phone was ring-ing. He took the call. "Antonio, it's for you."

Antonio shouldered the phone as he opened the phone

and removed the small chip that allowed the phone to be re-routed. He started jumping up and down and said, "I'm on my way."

He turned to me. "Joseph and Alen are our suspects . . . they're working in the kitchen with Toppy. He's absolutely slammed . . . but he's keeping them busy until I get there. We got a whole cruise ship that arrived on the island. I've got to get there. I must apprehend these guys, interview them, and get them off Capri as soon as possible. Now . . . did you see how I took this out?"

I nodded. "Leave it with me."

He grinned. "I leave it in capable hands. Nice hickey, Marius." He touched my throat at the seam of my shirt collar. I'd thought I had the thing well hidden.

"Crisanto's a frisky one." Alex grinned.

Crisanto. The mere mention of his name did wobbly things to my cock. I took a deep breath and focused on my electronic broom. I also had to get on with the business of hunting out bugs. As the morning wore on, two more rooms emptied out, and apart from some disgusting bedroom habits, I didn't find anything I needed to report to the police. One guy, for example, had a semen fetish, or was it a condom fetish? He'd left all his used rubbers tied off and lined up on his pillow. *Charming.*

Another guy had obviously been fishing and cleaned and gutted his catch in the bathroom, leaving the stinky entrails in the sink.

"You wouldn't believe some of the things I've seen," Alex told me.

"What's the worst?"

"You don't want to know. Oh, there was one guy who left eighty wooden legs," he said with a laugh."

"Eighty?"

"Yeah. And they were all left legs."

We both laughed over that one.

"It's one of the risky parts of online bookings," he said. "There are some real fruitcakes out there."

His cell phone rang. It was Antonio. His team had been able to apprehend both Alen and Josep with a struggle that apparently wrecked some of Toppy's kitchen.

"They've admitted they hit Signore Brusco's store." Alex looked so upset as he relayed all of this to me. "He is getting them off the island, but Zeca's having a really bad time at the café."

"I can be there in fifteen minutes," I said, "If that helps."

"It does," Alex said. "Lookit, now that Alen and Josep are out of the way, I can keep doing sweeps of the rooms . . . and if there's any trouble I'll call you."

"Good deal."

I knew I had shorts and a T-shirt back in Crisanto's room, but when I knocked there was no response. I tried his cell phone, but it went to voice mail. My house key was in his room. I heard his sudden laughter and looked up to find him wearing a tiny white swimsuit on the balcony of another room. The penthouse. He was sipping coffee with a man I recognized.

Ah . . . this had to be the famous fashion designer, but I couldn't place him.

Then . . . I tried not to freak out.

When I called out and waved, Crisanto's companion pointed to me.

"I need to get my things," I told him.

"Be right down."

He didn't move a muscle, and I started to fidget. I was worried about Zeca, and I needed to get changed. When he didn't look like he was going to come down, I went to find Alex.

"I've got stuff to lend you." None of his tennis shoes really fit me well enough for me to run around in them and we were in a hurry. "Are flip-flops okay?" he asked anxiously.

I groaned. They wouldn't be the most comfortable things to work in, but they would have to do.

"You look upset," Alex said.

"Yeah. A little." It had been a long time since I'd been left without a thing to wear. Oh, for the days of my on-set dresser. She'd been a peach, Annie had . . .

"Listen, Jose, the designer . . . he's been after Crisanto to do a fashion line for him . . . a sports line for men," Alex said. "It could be very lucrative for both of them. This is actually the reason Crisanto came here."

"Really, how do you know all this?"

"Crisanto booked his room around Jose's visit. He deliberately asked me not to put them too close to one another. He said he wasn't into the party scene."

"Oh, okay." I nodded stiffly. That made me feel better, but he was still behaving like an ass. At least I had my wallet on me.

"I can get your stuff out of his room once he gives me permission," Alex said. "I'll have someone drop the key and your clothes over at the café."

"You don't mind?"

He smiled. "You've turned out to be a fucking godsend. Of course I don't mind. I'd give you my copy of the house key but Hugh's got it, and he's down at the dock buying fresh fish for the hotel."

"No problem," I said.

As I left, I stole a look at the upstairs balcony, but they had moved indoors. I could hear their laughter. I felt like the poor neighborhood kid pressing his nose up to the bakery window.

I had to get over the idea he was having rampant sex in there. Unfortunately, I was the possessive type. Always had been. It hadn't been helpful in any of my relationships, and it looked like I wasn't about to change anytime soon. I heard a fresh burst of laughter and walked away from the sound.

It hurt me that he'd virtually ignored me. I didn't care how hot this deal was. I wouldn't have left him standing around waiting. I thought about all the things we'd done in bed, and I felt stupid. Really stupid.

I changed out of my borrowed clothes. "I'll leave them in the closet here for you in case you need them later," Alex told me. I left the hotel and was almost at the restaurant when Crisanto caught up with me.

"What do you think?" he asked, putting his hand on my shoulder.

"What do I think about what?"

"These." He stood back and let me get an eyeful of his white running pants with a lilac and red trim. The matching T-shirt fit him like a glove.

"Very nice. I have to go. I have to work."

"Wait . . .are you angry?"

"Yes, I am. I . . .you know what? I don't have time for this now. My family's under attack, I have the worst fucking shoes in the world on my feet, and I'm about to spend the day running myself ragged. But do you care? No. You don't give a shit!"

"I didn't know." He looked me up and down. "I told you I'd be right down. I was in the middle of a conversation. An important one. Why are you working in the café again?"

"You might as well know they found the culprits behind the thefts in the hotel and the shop vandalism."

"What shop vandalism?"

My head hurt. I was tired, and I had to go. "We'll talk later."

"No. We'll talk now. Why are you so upset with me? If it's the shoes . . . you can have mine. I think they'll fit. We're around the same size."

He began peeling off the socks and shoes. He was being very nice,and I was in a pissy mood.

"I'm doing a clothing line with Jose de la Jacinto," he said. "I can still hardly believe it."

"Believe it. He's lucky to have you." I tried to be nice. All I could think, though, was that Alen and Josep had wrecked Uncle Toppy's kitchen. I got my feet into the shoes, and he took charge of the flip-flops.

"Good thing I'm not playing soccer," he said. "Can I see you later?"

"Yes." I nodded. "And thanks."

"Por nada. It's nothing." He blew me a kiss and darted back the way he'd come. I had to laugh as I heard the slap of the flip-flops against the old, cobbled road.

I hadn't been in the café five minutes when I got the full horror of the shop vandalism. Zeca was doing his best to remain calm but Angie, Uncle Toppy's fiancée was sobbing in the kitchen. She'd come to help, but she was a wreck.

"Signore Brusco is her father," Zeca told me. "She's taken the attack on him very, very hard. He and his partner, Signore Beppe, adopted her when she was five. She loves them and can't handle what happened to them."

"I don't blame her." I looked around at all the food in the kitchen. Alen and Josep had apparently gone berserk flinging food at the arresting officers. One food mixer was destroyed but other than that . . . nothing else seemed broken, but . . . it was still a shambles.

"Why don't I clean up?" I asked. "You go make your coffees, and I'll get things going in here." I sounded more confident than I felt.

"Bless you," Zeca said. "We have two night staff workers coming in a couple of hours. I called them, but they can't be in until our lunch session begins. They're working as life-guards down at the beach. Today of all days!"

I nodded. Life was like that. I looked at poor, beautiful Angie leaning against the sink with a dishcloth in her hand. She looked disheveled but if anything, even more beautiful in her grief. I didn't even know her father, and I had to hold the tears back.

"He saved me," she said. "My mother . . . she was . . . you know . . . a puttana. She used to beat me . . . put me out of the house at night so she could entertain men. He saved me. He fed me. They took care of me. He paid her a lot of money so he could adopt me. He and Papa . . . My fathers . . . they are wonderful men. Why would anyone hurt them?"

I put my arms around her. "I don't know, Angie. There are sick people in this world."

She kept sobbing and then I heard a knock at the kitchen door. We sidled over so I could open it. Hugh stared past us, his expression growing into one of horror when he saw the mess.

"Holy fuck!" he shrieked. "I'll kill those . . . bastards!"

"Yes!" Angie's tears suddenly evaporated. "I kill them, too!"

"Steady on there," Hugh said. "Put the knife down, Angie." He wrestled the implement she'd suddenly picked up out of her grip.

He looked at me. "Can you cope?"

"Not really. And we're gonna need food, but I have no idea what and how much."

He thrust a paper package in my arms. "Your fish for the day. Stick it in the fridge. When Alex gets over here, he can start preparing them. I'm going back to the hotel. I'm gonna send him and a couple of my chefs over here."

Angie suddenly grabbed a giant wooden spoon that hung on the wall.

"I'm going to avenge my fathers!" she announced dramatically and marched out of the café.

"Are you having fun in Capri yet?" Hugh deadpanned and took off at a run.

I rolled up my proverbial sleeves and got busy. The two thieves had thrown jars of oil and marinated antipasto . . . I fell over twice in the slippery goo. A good going-over with the mop and some bleach helped, but I was seriously short of food. I tried not to panic.

Zeca came in and whipped up a few omelets, shouting, "We need onions, tomatoes, pancetta!"

"On it," I said and began chopping. I ran over to the sink where Angie had left her bread. If a simple phone call had disturbed her baking efforts, her father's attack had positively demolished it. The bread was hard as a rock. All four loaves in the basket would make handy weapons but were virtually inedible.

"Alex is bringing some from the hotel," Zeca told me. He gave me a stern look. "Don't tell Angie."

Once the floor was clean and the chopping done, I tackled the dishes and glassware piled up on tables and the serving counter out front.

Zeca kept thanking me and then . . . blessed relief, help arrived.

Alex took over in the kitchen with two chefs. I took orders, but that soon proved to unglue the kitchen staff. We were out of many things, and the chefs started turning out whatever they felt like serving . . . with often hostile results.

"What's this? I wanted eggs," the customers would huff.

"It's a sandwich. It's good for you," would be my response.

At least the sandwiches were good . . .

People kept coming in all day just to gossip about Alen and Josep. By now the news had gone around that they had been responsible for Signore Brusco's attack. I was thrilled that nobody mentioned the hotel. The less said about the unfortunate occurrences there, the better. Some seemed to know about the store's vandalism . . . others had their own stories of how anti-gay the owners seemed, which was weird when they were an obviously gay couple.

Soon people were embellishing, calling them Soviet spies. It was ridiculous. Small town gossip could be so vicious. People would stay for coffee and not leave.

Uncle Toppy came in at noon. He'd been at Signore Brusco's store, helping him clean up. He put his arms around me and Zeca.

"We're all going over there tomorrow morning when his new windows arrive, and we're going to have a dress shop party, okay? Until his place is up and running, tomorrow we stay closed."

Zeca and I nodded.

"Are you doing okay here?" he asked surveying the mess that was now his café.

He seemed to take it in stride. "This is nothing. You should see us on New Year's," he told me.

Around two o'clock, I realized we were so slammed we hadn't even had time to prepare the lunches. There was a line outside the restaurant and people were standing in the doorways with coffees, Italian sodas, and gelatos.

"God help me," Zeca said. "I never want to see another cup of coffee again!"

I became aware of a shift in the energy of the café.

"Your boyfriend's here," Zeca whispered. He dropped to the floor and lay on his back.

Crisanto strolled in, Henry in tow. He was walking with his usual languid gait, but I saw the flicker of desire in his eyes. My cock did the happy dance in my shorts.

"Hello, handsome," I said, which was about the most unsuave thing I could have said.

"Hello, you." His eyes twinkled at me. I had the sudden urge to grab him to me, cover his face with kisses and suck his cock. Not necessarily in that order.

"This is a mob scene." Henry was looking around.

"Chaos," Crisanto agreed. "We came to help. What do you need?"

"What do you know about espresso machines?" Zeca asked, getting to his feet. Henry and Crisanto exchanged odd looks.

"We've known each other since my days playing for Milan," Crisanto said. "We owned a restaurant there. He's good with the coffee. I'm better with taking food orders."

"You make coffee?" Zeca asked.

Henry shrugged. "Not as good as yours but—"

"Please," Zeca begged, "If you could make a few coffees . . . I need to get to the kitchen." He turned to Crisanto. "If you could help Marius take a few orders I'm going to check on my wayward kitchen hands. They were supposed to be up from the beach by now."

"Yeah, that's why we're here," Crisanto said. "Antonio's men arrested them. Your kitchen hands got drunk down at the beachfront. Apparently, a couple of ladies showed up with champagne and um . . . ." He grinned. "Some nudity became involved."

"Drunk?" Zeca stared at him. "But Capri has no nude beaches."

"I guess they decided otherwise."

"Are you kidding me right now?"

"No. I spoke to Antonio . . ." Crisanto spread his hands. "He called me at the hotel. He asked us to come straight here and tell you. He's down at the beach heading back to Naples. He's had more crime here in two days than the island's had in decades! Apparently, all his phone calls to your cell go to voice mail, and the café's calls go through to some porn site."

"They . . . what?"

"I'll fix the phones," I said. Zeca looked like he was going to fall down again.

We all got busy. I bumped into Crisanto a few times, but I took it as a pleasurable experience, not unwelcome at all.

He cornered me just outside the kitchen.

"I keep trying to run into you just to touch you. Haven't you even noticed?" He looked dejected.

"Yeah. I noticed. Come into the pantry with me. I want a word with you."

He laughed as I jumped on him and planted my lips on his. I backed him against a shelf filled with cans of peas and dropped my face to his track pants. I nuzzled him and heard the tsking sound that escaped his lips.

"Not here, baby," he started to say, but his body betrayed him.

I got to my knees, keeping one foot far back against the door, blocking anyone entering. When I took his cock out, his hands flew around my head. I began to suck him voraciously. He banged back against the shelf, cans falling down around us. I didn't care. I want what I wanted. He tried to catch some and also tried to hold my head to him.

His cock was huge, and it was still taking some getting used to. Long and thick, my mouth fitted around him, but it took a lot of work sucking in his length. His juices were sweet, however. I kept him where I wanted him by holding his balls tightly in my grip. Somebody was at the pantry door.

"Marius is that you in there?"

"Yes, we won't be long," Crisanto's voice rasped.

"Are you having a quickie?" Zeca was giggling now. I'd never heard my cousin giggle. It must have been hysteria.

"Are they doing it?" another voice asked. "I wanna see."

"Shut up," Zeca said, "let's get back to work."

I did not slacken the pace or pressure on my new lover's cock. He was flailing as I started squeezing tighter on his ballsack.

"Oh, oh, oh!" He fucked my face, his cockhead seeming to grow wide, bigger . . . God help me he was gonna choke me to death with that beautiful thing. He pumped harder, faster. He grabbed my ears and apologized.

"I just want you so bad." My name came out a low moan. "Mariusssssss."

Gulping down his juices I rocked back on my haunches, gazing up at him.

"Fuck," he said. "Just when I think it can't get any hotter between us."

He leaned down, his cock falling from my open mouth. He held my face and kissed me. He helped me up, and I kissed him again. Now I was ready to work. As we busted out of there, Hugh was grinning at us.

"We've all christened the pantry," he said.

"Sorry you missed the party," Crisanto joked. He helped me grab plates, and we rushed back to our tables.

At five thirty, we shooed out the last of the café's patrons. A few mumbled that Crisanto and I were mean because we tried to force them to order sandwiches, but the truth was, the chefs had begged us to push them. Nobody sent them back because they were so damned good. We locked the doors and pretended to ignore the plaintive faces pressed up against the windows. Toppy and Angie insisted we all sit down.

Zeca, Alex, Hugh, Henry, Crisanto, the chefs from Hotel Bello, and I were now Toppy's guests. We pushed several tables together and sat, chattering like chickens.

Angie and Toppy went off to the kitchen, and I could smell something really good cooking back there. They returned a little while later with the man Angie introduced to us as Signore Brusco.

I instantly loved him. The small, elegant, white-haired man and his life partner, Signore Beppe, were possibly the most handsome men I'd ever met. They'd brought a few wine bottles from their private collection.

"My God," Henry whispered to me. "That bottle of Giacomo Conterno Barolo Monfortino . . . it's like four hundred dollars a bottle."

Evidently, Signore Beppe heard him and smiled. "Have you ever tasted it?"

Henry shook his head. "Only in my fantasies."

"Then you must try it!" The man stood and came over to us, pouring the wine in an expert way. "This is one of our favorites, made from a little grape called the nebbiolo."

He stood back, anxious for our responses. He couldn't have wished for better. The wine was smooth, velvety, and had a spicy . . . almost wild berry flavor.

"This is delicious," Crisanto enthused, "and I usually don't drink wine."

In deference to the two signores, Toppy gave them seats at the head of the table. They were utterly beguiling with each of us. They charmed me with their warmth. They knew how to engage each and every one of us. They asked Henry about his book. I think my favorite moment came when Signore Beppe pointed to Crisanto and stood and mimed kicking a soccer ball.

Everybody laughed.

Signore Beppe put his fingers to his lips and kissed them to the air.

Crisanto looked delighted. We exchanged smiles, his hand going to my leg under the table.

And then Antonio arrived. He looked happy but exhausted.

"The kitchen hands are sleeping off their morning of champagne on the beach. They promise to be here tonight," he announced with a grin. "Fully clothed."

I loved watching the way he kissed everybody's cheeks twice, then kissed Zeca on the mouth. We toasted one another and dug into the best pasta I've ever eaten in my life.

I recognized it immediately, and my heart did the samba in my chest.

"Oh!" I said. "It's *bottarga con fregola*! You first made me this dish when I was five years old, and we were all in Sardinia, do you remember, Uncle Toppy?"

"That's where I learned this dish. I can't believe you remember that!"

"Those were the happiest days of my life, when we were one big, happy family."

Our eyes met. I felt overcome with emotion.

"Thank you, family," Signore Brusco said.

"Family!" we all chorused, raising our glasses.

"Is that fish roe I taste?" Crisanto asked.

"Dried fish roe. It's a Sardinian specialty," Toppy told him.

"You know," Crisanto drawled. "You're an excellent chef. You should really open a restaurant."

Everybody laughed. We all talked at once about the crazy day, the ridiculous rumors, the sandwiches we had pressed on people . . .

"You watch," Toppy said. "They will all be asking for sandwiches tomorrow."

Antonio filled us all in on arresting Alen and Josep.

"They were jealous of Alex and Zeca," he said. I could tell that really infuriated him. "Jealous of their happiness . . . their partners, their family . . . even their relationship with

Toppy. They resented Alex and Hugh opening a hotel. They seemed to forget the hard work they have both put into it."

"Some people just enjoy blaming others for their own failings, but at least we stopped them." Toppy held up his glass. "To love!" he said.

"To love," we all shouted back.

I didn't think I could remember a time when I felt love more . . . ever . . . in my life.

CHAPTER SEVEN

Crisanto and I could hardly wait to get back to his room. "I wasn't in a hurry to return your belongings, in case you didn't know," he told me. "I like having your things there. That's why I didn't rush down this morning."

"Well," I said, "I am glad you told me." He had the cutest way of bumping into me like he had in the restaurant . . . his way of publicly touching me. I enjoyed bumping him back.

At the hotel, we went to his room where he threw me on the bed. With the doors open to the terrace, the sound of the house guitarist singing from the banyan tree downstairs by the pool, Crisanto's hot mouth on my cock . . . man, this was heaven. I had to have died and gone there; only somebody forgot to tell me.

He worked my body with his tongue. He loved to lick a man's ass. I could tell he couldn't wait to eat me . . . but then he got this wild-eyed look. I knew he had to fuck me. He reached for his box of rubbers. The maid had moved them. That was a funny moment. We found them, and I was pleased to say it didn't kill the mood.

Crisanto's mouth was back on mine. I could taste wine and Toppy's Sardinian pasta on his tongue as he rolled the rubber over his cock and started sliding against me. The good sensations pulsed to swift and sharp pain as he entered me. I knew it would ease, but his was the biggest cock I'd ever had, and we'd gone at it for hours the night before. Sheets of white, blinding firelight shot across my brain.

He stopped. "Am I hurting you?"

112

I nodded. It was agony, but I still wanted him.

"We'll take it slow," he said when I gripped his hips, letting him know I wanted him.

When he finally immersed himself inside me, my whole body vibrated with joy. I was excited that the guitarist was singing 'Dolce Far Niente' . . . Ah, yes, it was so sweet to do nothing more than let Crisanto fuck me gently . . .

He rocked his cock inside me. He took his time. It hurt when he withdrew but felt so amazing when he pushed back again. My body clung to him. I started to come, my ass muscles clenching down on him. He came with a roar, my legs wrapping themselves around him . . .

Crisanto collapsed on top of me but stayed inside me, whispering my name like a chime in the wind, making me get hard again . . .

We made love all night, running down to the pool long after sunset, to swim.

Crisanto was not one to talk about himself much, but he told me he'd grown up poor and that his professional soccer earnings had allowed him to support his mother and two sisters. I was surprised to learn he still sent them money each month.

"One of my sisters is married . . . she found herself an absolute bum. I send her money . . . and my mother, she lives in a big house now, so they live with her."

He told me the family was in Salvador da Bahia, on the northeastern coast of Brazil. "It is the most beautiful city. They call it the bay of all saints. I call it the city of many colors because every house is so brightly painted. And I think you will love the smell."

"The smell?" I grinned. "What is it?"

"It is on the air. It is in the skin, the clothing. *Acarajé.*"

I repeated the name. "What is it?"

"Bean and shrimp fritters. I miss them every day."

I believed him. The faraway look in his eyes pained me. He'd had to go a long way from his city of many colors to make his fortune.

"You'll see it," he said. "I think you'll like it. And I think you will soon miss *acarajé*, too."

A few minutes later he broke the tender mood by telling me that he had only three more days in Capri. Three days, two nights. I was going to miss him. We didn't talk of the future, but in spite of how good I felt with him, my sleep was troubled. He'd told me he didn't do serious relationships. He was all about fun.

And yet . . .

In the morning, he awoke me with kisses, a mind-blowing blowjob that reached all the way to my toes . . . and then he began to talk about the future. Over coffee and rolls on his terrace, he told me he wanted to see me again.

"I have to go back to Genoa. I start training Saturday. Can you come visit me for a few days?"

"Yes," I said. "I would love it."

"I would love it if you were at the first match next Sunday. I am really worried about that one."

"Of course I'll be there." The thought of not waking up with him every day was horrible. He asked me what I'd done about the apartment building in Athens. I admitted that I hadn't contacted the attorney Toppy had suggested.

"We need to rectify the problem there," he said.

We? That kind of gave me a lift. He wanted the phone number Toppy had given me.

"I want to Google this attorney," he said. "I want to make sure this is a good guy for you to work with."

I was touched that he cared so much, and I handed him the slip of paper Toppy had given me.

He had a meeting with the designer upstairs, so after a

quick shower together, I borrowed a pair of his running pants and a T-shirt and went to meet my family at the dress shop.

"I'll call you," Crisanto promised.

Down in the lobby, the hotel seemed to be back on course with no more dramas. As I joined Alex and Hugh and walked over to Signore Brusco's, I could tell that my cousin was much happier and relaxed now.

At the store, we all got busy. Zeca and Antonio joined us, and we made quick work of it. Toppy and Antonio installed the new cash register. By noon, we were done painting, and the new carpet would go in the following day. With the new windows installed, the place looked great.

Our two silver foxes said they were going to rest on their terrace with coffee and thanked us for our time. After a swift exchange of hugs, we walked back to Toppy's, where he opened up and immediately began pretending the cappuccino machine was broken.

I worked a busy shift, relieved that things were more or less back to normal . . . until I received a phone call from Crisanto, telling me he had an important business meeting with Jose de la Jacinto that night. I thought they'd had a meeting that day, but business was business. I knew nothing about fashion. As an actor, I'd always worn what I was told to wear.

As a civilian, so far, I wasn't showing much of a flair for knowing what to wear. I had mismatched socks on my feet and borrowed clothing from Crisanto.

"Can I see you tomorrow?" he asked.

"Of course," I said. Sadness enveloped me. I had to get a grip on myself. I wanted to ask why we couldn't see each other after the meeting, but the truth was we'd spent a lot of time together, and he was here on business.

I went home for a wonderful siesta and found that my

room was comfortable and relaxing. I went for a walk as the sun set and spotted a charming restaurant built into the mountainside. I wondered if I'd need reservations and stared up at it. I liked that it was away from the town center and embarked on the long climb up to Le Grottelle.

A woman who insisted I call her Mama greeted me in the doorway of the little restaurant that resembled a well-appointed cave. She said she had a table waiting for me. She charmed me, asking what I wanted to eat.

"Pizza," I said.

She put me at an outdoor table and kept beaming at me as she brought me fresh bread and olive oil for dipping. A man came to me asking a million questions about how I liked my pizza. He too was adorable and twenty minutes later brought me the most wonderful caprese pizza piled high with mozzarella, tomato, and fragrant basil leaves. He gave me a glass of red wine that was the perfect accompaniment.

The restaurant filled quickly and became loud and raucous, but I didn't care. Somebody else had made the pizza set before me, and I wouldn't have to lift a finger to help clean up. When I paid my bill and stood to leave, I thought Mama might cry.

I let her hug me, and even the patrons waved goodbye. My path home was quicker than my arrival, and I returned to Toppy's house.

A quick check of my cell phone messages revealed that nobody missed me or needed to speak to me. I fell asleep on top of my bed, one shoe off, the other dangling from my big toe.

The next day, I received a text message from Crisanto, asking to meet me at Toppy's for a coffee at around noon.

Leaving town, he wrote. *Want to see you.*

I wasn't sure if this was good or bad . . . but cleaned and

washed the clothes he'd lent me and slipped them into a shopping bag with his running shoes.

He was already there when I arrived, wearing the same outfit I'd first seen him in. He had all his bags with him.

"I'm leaving this afternoon," he told me. "I'll call you. I want you to come to Genoa to visit me."

He could have just left . . . could have texted me a farewell, or not even said goodbye. He seemed preoccupied, and I had a terrible feeling something had gone wrong. He didn't want to talk about it, however.

"I'll call you," he said. He kissed my cheeks Italian style, and he was gone.

"Is he okay?" Zeca asked when I carried our cups—he'd barely touched his coffee—when I came back inside.

"I don't know."

"Yeah. Alex said he seemed upset. Listen I think he really likes you. He'll call."

"Thanks, Zeca." I meant it.

And, he did call. He called that night to tell me he was back in Genoa. He called me the next morning. He told me in minute detail all his activities. It was quite endearing, actually. He kept asking what I was doing. I began a new routine of writing in the mornings, swimming, working in the café, and then roaming the island with whoever was around afterward.

Antonio and Zeca took me to the other side of the island where I explored the definitely un-touristy side of the island of Anacapri. We rode the chair lift that covered half the island.

I was surprised to learn this part of the island had its own police force, and a rivalry existed between both.

Antonio revealed the other cop in Anacapri was determined to find the dog poop culprit himself. Antonio laughed about it, but I knew it really bugged him.

With the exotic flurry of having Crisanto at the Hotel Bello, I, like Cinderfella, came crashing back to reality with a massive thud. I had most evenings at Uncle Toppy's alone. I'd pick up something at the café or sit at one of the outdoor tables at my new favorite pizzeria, Al Buco, in Anacapri.

I loved people watching and came to adore their version of the caprese pizza. Somehow, Crisanto always managed to call as I was walking home from Toppy's or finishing the last bite of pizza at Al Buco.

One night he called as I was eating. "Take a photo and send it to me," he said. I chuckled and did as he asked.

He then apparently called the restaurant and paid my check. That surprised me.

"Why are you alone?" he asked me. "My God . . . I am going crazy thinking about some other guy asking you out."

"I like you," I said. "Besides . . . I'm not alone. I hang out with my cousins . . . but they're in love. They work long days. They want their evenings with their lovers."

"Then you should come here," he said. "I'm playing soccer on Sunday. Maybe you want to invite Antonio and Zeca to come with you?"

"Where do you suggest we stay? I don't know Genoa."

"You'll stay with me," he huffed. "Of course!"

When I mentioned the idea to Antonio, he was over the moon. He was such a huge Genoa fan, and I liked the idea of traveling with him and Zeca.

The three of us spent all of Monday hunched over our laptops . . . and it was a little dismaying to learn that if we flew from Naples to Cristoforo Colombo Airport in Genoa, it would be around three hundred and thirty Euros, or four hundred US dollars for each roundtrip ticket. A lot for a short flight.

Alternatively, train-travel was around thirty dollars but would take almost a day. Crisanto had called begging me to stay for a week. Of course, I agreed. It had been over a week since I'd seen him, and I missed him terribly.

I threw caution to the wind and booked three tickets on an Alitalia flight for all three of us. It was my gift to Antonio and Zeca, who couldn't believe it. They were going to spend a couple of days with us, then go back to Naples to visit Antonio's mum. I would stay with Crisanto then come back to Capri at the end of the week.

On Saturday morning, we flew in to Genoa ... And I couldn't wait to see him.

As a surprise, Crisanto met us at the airport in his black convertible, football jerseys for all of us. Half the people I knew in Europe called the game soccer, half called it football. The half-red, half-blue Genoa jerseys seemed apt somehow. They were nicknamed rossoblu I learned. The animal emblem was a griffin.

"They say this is where J.K. Rowling received her inspiration for the house of Gryffindor," Crisanto told us.

He kissed my cheeks quickly, and we jumped in the car. I could see people pointing to him, snatching pictures. He was obviously well-known here. He negotiated the streets of the seaport town like a pro, his hand constantly reaching for mine when he wasn't shifting gears.

Antonio was like a big kid. We arrived at the Stadio Luigi Ferraris soccer field, where he changed into shorts and soccer shoes and ran around the field with the team, which was in final practice.

Zeca and I grinned like idiots, watching them from the stadium seats. He suddenly gripped my hand.

"It's so wonderful to see you smiling. It's been breaking my heart to see you so sad."

"Drat the luck," I joked. "And I thought I was doing such a good job hiding it."

"You are, sweetie. I just know you . . . and I know he's missed you, too." He gripped my hand harder. "You do know Antonio turns into a lunatic at a soccer game, don't you?"

"Half of Europe does," I said.

"No . . . his inner hooligan flies his freak flag—high—you might never want to talk to him again."

"My dad's embarrassed me at soccer matches since I was a toddler," I assured him. "Which is why I stopped following the sport."

"Your honey's looking at us."

We dropped each other's hand and began to wave. Indeed, I kept finding Crisanto's gaze seeking mine as the practice match went on. I hadn't expected such a big soccer field or the fans that kept burrowing their way past security people to reach the wire fencing begging the players for their autographs. When Antonio came over to us, his eyes sparkled. "This time tomorrow twenty-thousand people are going to be here," he said. "What a gift this was. Thank you so much, Marius."

"Don't thank me. Thank Lucky Pants on the field there."

"Lucky Pants?" He started to laugh. "Nice nickname for one of the best strikers in the history of the game."

Lord . . . I didn't even know what a striker was. I began to feel terrible. Poor Crisanto . . . having a lover who knew nothing about his game. And then my cell phone rang.

"It's him," I said. "Texting me."

"From the field?" Antonio slapped his thigh in glee.

It was three XXXs, but it might have been a six-page sonnet. I loved it. I sent some kisses back. He'd been off to the side pretending to sip water when he sent the text. I looked across the field and caught his glance and his wicked grin.

"I took lots of photos of you." Zeca showed Antonio his digital images.

"Oh, boy. Look at me kicking a ball to Marco Rossi and Crisanto Alvarenga!"

As we watched the practice go on, I was struck by how handsome, and expressive all the players were. They yelled at each other, kissed each other . . . they were hilarious.

When practice was over, Crisanto ran over to us. He was drenched with sweat.

"Come on," he said. "We go home, shower and change, then we have dinner some place really special."

His apartment was in the city center, which I learned only allowed cars that traveled within its confines by permit. It gave the UNESCO-protected historical area an even more authentic feel to it, seeing so many people walking. We had to park in a special lot and walk to his apartment a few blocks over. The narrow streets charmed me. It was like Capri on a bigger scale. I could see the city stretching toward the ocean on our left. The buildings were ancient and gorgeous. There was a ruined, yet burnished feel to it all. I could hear the faint echoes of poets, artists, writers, lovers . . . I could hear those still living and those in repose.

"I know," he said, watching me. "You feel the power of this place, too."

His apartment was located inside a sixth-century palace, one of the many he told us that had been built during that time. It overlooked the city square, that, he told us had centuries of stories to tell.

There was a huge outdoor café, and from what I glimpsed, a host of expensive shops clustered around it.

"This is the original door colonnade," he told us. "All these floors made of slate and marble are original, too."

"I don't see dog poop anywhere," Antonio said, sounding suddenly depressed. "I'm never going to catch the person who's ruining my island."

We lugged our things up to Crisanto's spacious, two-level

dwelling that had Juliet windows from the kitchen and two of the three bedrooms overlooking the square.

"Make yourselves at home," he told Antonio and Zeca, leading them to a lovely room near ours. "I need to spend a few minutes with Marius."

"Take your time," Antonio said. "We'll keep ourselves busy."

I'd never seen Crisanto sweaty. Not really. He was a very fastidious, clean man who showered immediately after every run. I loved the smell of his soaked skin and hair. I sucked on a strand hanging over his eyes. I'd never been jealous of hair before.

He kissed me, his fingers tearing at my clothing before we'd even closed the door. He moaned into my mouth.

"You stayed away too long," he said.

I felt his cock hardening against my hand as I rubbed at his wet shorts. I took all his kisses and wanted more. He pushed me onto the bed. The last thing I saw was him, naked, his cock jutting at me as he flipped me onto my belly. My cock rubbed against the bedspread as his face delved into my ass. I lifted the lower half of my body, longing for his tongue against me. He didn't disappoint.

"All your hickeys are gone," he said. "I need to tattoo you personally."

"No need," I assured him, looking over my shoulder at him. "I'm right here."

He prepared me for him with his tongue and first one finger, then a second. By the time he slid the rubber on and worked his way into me, my body remembered all the pleasure he'd given it before. He did things to me from this position no man had ever done before. Each time he fucked me this way the pleasure was indescribably intense.

God . . . I was going to come already. He must have anticipated this because he reached under and grabbed me, urging me to an incredible orgasm. He leaned back and begged me to turn over.

Still embedded in me, he kept fucking me.

"I love how hard you are," he said. His taut belly rubbed against me. He pushed my legs back, wanting closer entry. He was so deep inside me. I could feel his cock pushing against my stomach. I met his thrusts as his mouth clamped over mine. He kissed me, moving his lips over my chin, nose, settling on my eyes, and moving back to my mouth. He started fucking me harder, and his breath came in shallow spurts.

He slipped his hand under my head and held me to him as he came, a heavy, shuddering climax, his teeth against mine, tongue against tongue, our hearts hammering with molten heat for one another.

"I don't know if this is a good time to mention it," he said after the fire blew out and we could breathe again, "but I'm falling in love with you, Marius. It scares me. It really does."

"I feel the same way, but I'm gonna do it. Be scared and still do it."

He stared down at me, fear and need mingling in his gaze. He didn't say anything, but he didn't have to. The words had been said. They may as well have been written. And it was. I felt a breeze carried on the wind from his opened windows. It had been carried like a letter on the wings of countless, ageless ghosts in this old, crumbling city that had already started to seep into my bones.

When we'd showered and changed, he turned to me.

"I bought something for you. I saw it a few days ago."

"You must be psychic. I adore presents."

He laughed. "Let's hope you adore this one." He held up a long red stick with a few bulges in it.

"I give up, what is it? Some kind of weird light bulb?"

"This is a vibrating butt plug. I insert it inside you and, all evening, I operate it via a remote control. I can make it go slow or fast. I can get you all hot and bothered. I can make you come."

"Oh, no," I said. "I want to relax and enjoy myself."

"You'll enjoy yourself, I promise." His fingers worked on the buttons of my jeans. He pushed me onto the bed, licking my ass. When he inserted his new toy, it didn't feel very comfortable. He yanked me to my feet and buttoned my jeans up again.

"You're not hard, Marius."

"No. it doesn't feel—"

Oh. My. God . . .

He'd switched the thing on. It buzzed deep inside my ass, and the sensations were . . . blissful.

"I can't have dinner like this."

"Yes, you can." He turned it off again. He was enjoying himself.

Bzzz . . . I almost choked. My ass was vibrating again.

He took us along his street, which was called Via XX Settembre, a name that tickled me. Twenty Septembers. He pointed out other palaces that went back as far as the one he lived in, but not all of which had been so carefully looked after.

Every now and then, my vibrator would wake up, and I'd start to sweat. The discomfort of walking around with the thing inside me had worn off, and I was in a constant state of anticipation and rampant horniness.

Sweat beaded on my face and neck as we kept walking, making it hard to concentrate.

I tried to focus as Crisanto showed us his favorite nooks and crannies in his neighborhood. Most of the ancient palaces had entrances in grubby, tiny alleyways the average tourist might balk at entering, but I felt very safe . . . with a cop and a soccer player.

"These streets are called *caruggi,* and they are some of the oldest from Medieval Europe," he said. When we stopped for dinner at Zeffirino, the waiters fawned all over him, offering us free grappa, the local wine, as we perused the menu. We let Crisanto choose our meals since apparently, he knew it by heart.

"How about the *mandilli de saea*?" he asked Antonio.

Bzzzz . . . I almost jumped out of my seat. Crisanto was a cool customer. He held a conversation with the wine steward while sending me on a rocket ship to the moon.

"Ah . . . the famous silk handkerchief pasta." Antonio grinned at Zeca. "We read about it online."

The pasta was simply incredible. Crisanto released me from the exquisite pressure when the food arrived. The homemade squares were prepared with a light pesto sauce that oozed garlic and goodness. I didn't usually like pesto sauce, but the basil was fragrant and light, the perfect choice for the admittedly silky pasta squares. We split two different kinds of fish and a huge salad that was mixed right in front of us, the dressing prepared on the spot.

"I know what I want for dessert," Crisanto said, winking at me.

Bzzz . . .

"Me, too," Antonio said. "I want that *mille foglie* I see over there."

"So romantic," Zeca teased.

Bzzzzzzzz . . .

"It's my sweet tooth," Antonio said.

I bolted from my seat into the restroom. I didn't have time to unbuckle my belt or undo the fly buttons on my jeans. Crisanto had increased the tempo, and my whole body was on red alert. I came hard, slumped against a urinal.

"I'm so gonna get him for this," I muttered.

Back home, he begged off any form of sex until the next

day.

"I will pleasure you, but I need to abstain for now. After the game," he said, "I'll want you very badly."

Fine by me. My ass was still tender from his little game, and I was happy to sleep in his arms. For some moments after he drifted off, his cheek against mine, I lay awake listening to his city. I enjoyed listening to the distant sound of car horns, even though they seemed so intrusive.

He had a smile on his face when I shifted in his tight embrace to steal a look at him. He was so beautiful. And he was here, right beside me. That put a smile on my face, and I soon fell asleep.

We were all up early the next day, but mine was the best wakeup call I'd had in almost two weeks. My lover's mouth was on me. He stroked me to an intense orgasm. He enjoyed making me come first thing . . . but for now, he preferred to wait.

My body was still in spasm mode when we went into the living room. Antonio was already wearing the team colors, and he looked ecstatic.

"What time do we leave?" he asked.

"Around noon," Crisanto said

"I'm so excited!"

Zeca who was sitting on a high stool at the breakfast island grinned at us. "I noticed you have pancetta and eggs in the fridge. I can also whip up some pancakes. Who's hungry?"

"Me!" we all shouted.

Cristiano seemed to be in buoyant spirits. His phone kept ringing with well-wishers calling to let him know they'd be watching the game. By the time we'd finished breakfast and Zeca and I were done loading the dishwasher, excitement had caught up with me. The doorbell rang. It was Henry and, Crisanto whispered to me, his apparent new boyfriend,

Alesso.

"He's a model and an actor," Crisanto said. The two men were very cute together.

My lover tugged me away from the group and into the bathroom.

"I can't wait," he said. "I must have you."

His cock sprang out at me the moment I opened his drawstring pants. I wanted to bathe him. Sucking him off in the shower was one of my favorite things to do, especially with the handheld showerhead mounted on the wall. He controlled the temperature and the mood as I knelt and sucked him. I loved his body. I cherished all the little wounds. He knew how and where he'd received each one.

"The one on your cheek and this one on your knee are my favorites," I told him.

I paused to reach down and kiss it.

"You have favorites? The others will be jealous," he said.

"But I have room in my heart for them all," I told him. I gazed up at him as I began to suck his cock. His raindrop setting had helped me inch back the silky, thin foreskin. I loved teasing it back from the head with my tongue, then drawing it back down with my lips. I knew it felt so good to him.

"Why do you favor the one on my knee?" he asked.

I released his cock for a moment. Cool water ran between us.

"You fell in the mud, broke your leg, and still won the game, and this is all there is to remember of it."

I kissed the knee again. He lifted my face, gazing down at me.

"You are such a poet. You must write. You and Henry . . . what am I to do with you both? I want you to write something I can read."

I nodded. "Let me suck your cock first."

He grinned. "Well, of course."

I put my mouth back on him, loving the difference between the cool water and his hot cock. I sucked on him, tugging his foreskin back with my mouth, pressing it back with my tongue. His cockhead glistened, and he seemed to jump as my mouth closed around him. I concentrated on keeping my whole mouth tight. He bucked against my tongue. I'd practiced sucking him in my mind, and I found deep breathing worked. He moved in and out of my mouth much easier now. I could tell it was driving him crazy.

He ran the rain fountain setting over his hair and down both our bodies. He let it run over my ass as I took him in deeper and deeper.

I had every inch of him in my mouth, and he began to fuck me gently. It didn't take him long to start going wild. I held his hips. He gripped the slick wall with one hand, the showerhead with the other. He jerked against me ... to me ... with me ... it was like riding a mechanical bull. I had to hang on. He came hard and deep in my throat.

He stood, plastered to the shower wall, the handheld head slipping from his grip. Raindrops fell on my feet as I sucked up every last drop of his come.

A team car picked us all up on the outskirts of the city. Crisanto was now tense and in full concentration. He was studying a game plan on his iPad, and we left him alone as he texted with his coach from his cell phone.

"This is going to be a tough game," he told us as we entered the stadium. "The last time we played Siena we lost four to one, and the fans booed us. They threw smoke bombs on the field."

"That was before you came along. You'll see, they'll be throwing you roses when this game's over," Antonio said.

My lover grinned. "From your mouth to the fans' ears."

He waved us all goodbye as he went one way and we entered the arena via the VIP entrance. Antonio was already in a mood to kill the fans of the Siena team. He was shouting and screaming and having a great time.

"Let's move," Zeca begged. "I can't bear it. The team isn't even on the field yet."

I personally got a kick out of it. Antonio was really letting all his pent-up aggressions out on the crowd.

When the teams ran onto the field, I got a sudden glimpse of what it must have been like in the old days with gladiators and knights entering fields.

My lover ran onto the field brandishing his team's flag high. I almost came in my pants when twenty-thousand people jumped to their feet roaring their approval as he stood in the middle and just kept the flag aloft.

"He's so wonderful," I said, tears coming to my eyes.

My mother chose that moment to text me. I saw it was her and shut the damned phone off. For the next two and a half hours, I was completely entranced by the game. And for the record, I only pretended I didn't know Antonio when he jumped over the fence and threatened to beat the umpire to death with his shoes.

I was relieved when Genoa won a hard-fought, exciting game, three to one.

"Didn't I tell you?" Zeca sighed. "And you know what? I still love him."

"Of course you do," I said.

"You're going to let him come back to more games, aren't you?" His eyes were wide with fear.

"If I come, he comes."

Zeca actually laughed. "You'll come," he said. "Crisanto is a man who's falling in love."

Over the next week, it sure felt that way. We spent every

minute together. It was hard to see Antonio and Zeca leave, but it also allowed me to focus purely on Crisanto. We couldn't go anywhere in Genoa without people congratulating him. In public, I was his friend, in private, he was all over me. He took me everywhere, to his favorite shipping village of Boccaddasse, an ancient, crumbling place where time seemed to have stood still. I loved it. We ate lunch at a small restaurant by the water's edge where we watched fishermen bringing in their haul and feeding tidbits to plump seabirds and rangy cats. We walked along the seawall, and he told me little stories about the area, about the legend of ghosts of sea captains' wives who haunted the area at night.

"Could you see yourself living here?" he suddenly asked. This was a loaded question, but I couldn't help saying yes. My answer hung in the wind like the clothes strewn across walkway clotheslines. I'd been honest, and that was all I could ask of myself. Each morning he planned our adventures around his weight-training sessions at the gym, isometric exercises with a man he called The Assassin, and his soccer practices. He wanted me with him all the time, and I was happy to go with him.

At the end of a perfect week, it was torture to leave him. And Genoa. I had a good cry in the shower alone. I didn't want Crisanto to see what an idiot I was, but he looked as unhappy as I felt. He gave me an oral assault in bed that I wouldn't soon forget, but at the airport, he gave me a mere lift of his hand in farewell and zoomed off to his gym session. He hadn't mentioned a return visit, and I tried not to be depressed about it as I boarded my flight to Naples.

CHAPTER EIGHT

Going back to Naples was hard, but the moment I landed I was delighted to see that I'd received a stream of text messages from Crisanto. As we taxied to the gate, I read through his sweet little notes.

It was so hard for me to see you leave . . .

I want to touch you all the time . . .

I hated watching you take those first steps away from me . . .

Balm for the soul . . . that's what they were. I fired back a quick text that I'd landed, and I missed him terribly.

Zeca and Antonio greeted me at the airport and took me to lunch where I sampled the city's famous fried pizza.

"Send me a photo," Crisanto said when he called. Of course, I did. When we walked back to Antonio's apartment, he asked to see photos of all the places I saw and even the meals I ate. He wanted to feel as though he were with me every moment. I found that endearing and dutifully took many pictures, sending them off to him.

"We should be there together," he told me.

"One day we will," I ventured.

"You bet I will. I thought I'd come to Capri for a few days after my game next Sunday. What do you think?"

"I think I can't wait."

We laughed together . . . the lightness . . . the joy was back. For both of us.

Our routine over the next few months slid into a sublime round of my visits to him and vice versa.

"We are a couple," he told me. "This is what you want, too, right?"

"Yes, yes."

"But we have to be discreet."

"Of course," I said.

Each time I went to see him play, I discovered new things about him. He was an emotional soccer player with deeply ingrained superstitions. He always kicked his first ball with his left foot. If he kicked with his right, the game would be bad. I had to confiscate his iPad when he went into soccer chat rooms and took it very hard when people criticized him.

I'd get him out of the apartment and drag him down Via Garibaldi. "Let's look at some really expensive underpants," I'd say, making him laugh as we walked in and out of outrageously priced boutiques.

He took me to the Galleria di Palazzo Bianco, or the Gallery of the White Palace, which turned out to be one of my favorite places. We loved to stand and observe the perfectly restored Baroque and Renaissance palaces, the galleries containing priceless pieces of art. We walked around the gardens, making up stories of what it must have been like, living here in the sixteenth century.

On one of our visits, we met a contessa, and she seemed to like us, inviting us to her home inside a Baroque palace inherited from her father's side of the family. Luisa was not beautiful. My father would have called her handsome. The beauty of her white-walled four-story palace struck me as we entered. I couldn't keep my gaze from the entryway as she ushered us into to the living room, overlooking the historical heart of the city. She offered me and Crisanto an apéritif, which I accepted to prolong the visit.

She mocked homosexual couples, then told us she adored them.

"This whole area was gay in the sixteenth century," she said. "They were all artists, scholars, and writers." I had no idea why she was telling us this, but suddenly she said, "I wish to sell this place. I want to move to Switzerland. If you know someone who wants to buy it and fix it up, let me know."

"Fix it up?" I asked still waiting for the offered cocktail, "But it's perfect."

She shook her head. "It is a shambles." Her expression turned morose. "I have sold ... lost, almost everything. What you see here is what I keep well maintained."

We didn't know what to make of her, and we never did get that cocktail.

As we walked home, Crisanto said, "Do you realize we never fight?"

I smiled. "That's a good thing, right?"

"Very good. I keep waiting for you to turn out to be a lunatic."

"I am a lunatic. Haven't you noticed yet?"

"No. Not like the dope addict we just visited. How would you feel about buying her palace and restoring it?"

I stopped walking. "Buy it?" I felt wary now. I'd made serious mistakes rushing into things with Paolo, and besides, my financial situation in Greece was on hold. We'd made contact with Toppy's attorney but had joined a long waiting list of people who wanted their day in an Athens court. "Well, I don't know."

"Think about it."

"I will." I turned to take another look at the palace we'd just left. Buying a palace! It seemed crazy.

He was watching me.

"I kind of ... I kind of love the idea," I said. "Can we really do it?"

"It means you have to move here." He smiled at me.

133

"I know, I know." I rolled my eyes. "We have to be discreet."

He shook his head. "I no longer worry about that. I worry about what you'll do here."

"I . . ." What would I do here?

The moment passed, and I realized he wanted me to think about the future. I would move here in a nanosecond if he wanted me to. He hadn't actually asked, and I just kept burying myself in my work at Toppy's each time I returned to the island.

"I'd write a book about the old palaces," I said, finally, just as we'd begun walking again.

His eyes lit up. "That's a wonderful idea. You are a very good photographer, and you could produce a beautiful book."

"I'm not a good photographer."

"Yes, you are, my love. I have each photo you've sent me of your meals." He grinned. "You have the gift."

He still didn't ask me to move to Genoa, but it was the closest we'd come to such a conversation. We walked home talking about the crazy contessa, and I marveled at the wonderful man I'd fallen in love with. This was the dreamiest relationship I'd ever had, and these priceless moments steeped in beauty helped me to remember when I was away from him, that it was true. It was all real.

"I think sometimes God makes the really good relationships take on an almost dreamlike quality when they have to be separated . . . it almost makes it easier," Zeca told me over coffee the next day.

That was the most beautiful thing he could have told me.

In the second week of September, Antonio received news that once he got his dognapper, he would be considered for his old job back in Naples.

"Funny thing is," he said when he came to help me and Zeca close up, "I don't want it anymore."

"Yes, you do," Zeca told him. "This is your dream. I want fried pizza for breakfast every morning. Don't take that away from me."

He winked at me. It was hard to imagine Capri without them. I'd have to get used to it, I supposed.

When Crisanto arrived a few days later in an unexpected visit, Antonio mentioned this to him, the idea that he no longer wanted the job in Naples.

"You say that now . . ." Crisanto laughed. "But I have a feeling about you. You're a pistol-packin' Pete."

That made us all laugh.

I loved that Crisanto had surprised me with a visit. I loved being part of the romantic couples strolling the starlit island, but first I dragged him up my nine million stairs to my room so I could show him how much I appreciated his thoughtfulness.

We reached the top, and he stepped right in a pile of pooh.

"What the . . ."

He stared down at his shoes. We took them off his feet and left them on the doorstep. We had some frisky business that needed our urgent attention.

Upstairs in my room, he was hard before I could edge his cock out of his pants.

"Fuck, I've missed you," he said, his mouth claiming mine as I tried valiantly to liberate him from the confines of all that fabric.

"You're not commando," I gasped, breaking off our kiss. It took all my efforts to remove the jeans and the tight black boxer briefs imprisoning him.

"No. Too uncomfortable in jeans." He lay back, eyes half closed, as I sucked his cockhead. "I love the smell of you and lemons. That to me is the smell of Capri."

"Me? What do I smell like?" I asked between licks and sucks.

"Sugar and sex."

I laughed. "That's what I smell like?"

"To me, yes. And it's my favorite smell in the whole wide world."

I ripped those underpants down and began sucking him in earnest. Each time we saw each other, our first forays into fucking were always hurried, insane ... perfect. It would take a day or so for us to calm down and take our time.

He pulled me up to him for kisses. Nobody kissed like he did. I could taste coffee and his apple gum on his breath.

As I slid back down his body, bathing every inch of him with my tongue, I sought out all the little bruises and scars that required my devotion. He moaned his approval, but soon, his jutting cock nudged the corner of my mouth.

I gave it the attention it so badly deserved, taking him inch by inch, deep into my throat. I moved off him, receiving a shout of protest until I opened his legs and began sucking his balls and ass.

He gripped the sheets, clutching handfuls as I worked him over with my tongue.

"Please," he groaned.

I reached up and sucked his cock. I knew he wanted to fuck me, but that would come next. I wanted to taste him, everything I'd been missing, and he came with a roar, yelling my name. We'd come a long way from furtive whispers in Toppy's kitchen pantry ...

We strolled the island as soon as we got our strength back. We couldn't decide where to eat and pondered our favorite options.

"If we were in Genoa, where would you want to go right

now?" he asked me suddenly.

"Oh, that's easy. Sciuscia and Sciorbi."

He grinned as I began to rhapsodize about our favorite new pizzeria and their fabulous pizza they called Fresh. Composed of red rocket, cherry tomatoes, and buffalo mozzarella, we'd become addicted to it.

"If we were home, that's exactly what I'd want to eat, too," he said, nodding approvingly.

I took a deep breath. "Do you go there without me?" I asked, surprised how much the idea upset me.

"No." He looked affronted. "Without you . . ." He blushed. "You want to know what I do?"

I nodded. "Tell me."

"Well, I order pizza from the place next to the scarf store. And then I eat it watching your show." He sighed. "I have made it through three years of episodes of *The Fletchers* on YouTube."

When I laughed, his expression grew pained. "You get more handsome as you get older," he said. "You were cute when the show started, but now, you are one hot chili pepper."

"Thanks," I said, surprised when he leaned in for a kiss.

My cell phone rang. I grimaced when I saw that it was my mother.

"Don't turn it off," he warned. "It's about time I got to know the woman who is so responsible for my happy state."

By now my mother knew about Crisanto and had been pushing to meet him. I'd fobbed her off with sundry excuses, but now he snatched the phone right out of my hands.

"But I'm hungry," I said. He ignored me.

He answered the call and the next thing I knew, he was inviting her and Dad to Genoa for his next soccer match.

"By the way," he said, as he ended the call, "we have a court date in October in Athens."

I nodded. I'd received an email, too, from the attorney, but I'd been so busy, and frankly, my mind so pleasantly occupied that I'd decided to deal with it later. We wandered off in search of pizza, and he grinned at me.

"You ever hear from the people who make your TV show?"

"Yeah," I said.

"Do they want you back?"

"I'm not going back. My life is here now."

"You don't miss acting?"

"Not at all. Maybe I'll go back to it someday." I hesitated.

"What?"

When I didn't respond, he stopped moving again. "Talk to me."

"I want to buy that palace. I think . . . I think the contessa would like us to have it."

He grinned. "Do you now?"

"I think we could fix it up and be so happy there."

"Marius, I think we would be happy anywhere."

That was true, too. He'd only recently admitted to me that his clothing line with Jose, the designer, fell apart because he wouldn't have sex with the guy.

"You given any thought to working with another designer?" I asked.

He glanced at me in the deepening night.

"Yes. But I won't do anything without you being there with me. I've had some offers, but they're not important now." He stared at me a moment.

"I just realized I invited your parents to Genoa, but Zeca and Antonio are coming this weekend. Do you think it's a problem?"

"Thank you for thinking of it. I . . . I don't know. Why don't we ask Zeca?"

"You never know." Crisanto shrugged. "Maybe this will

be a healing experience for everybody. You are my family here in Italy. I like to think we have one big, happy family here."

We found Zeca and Antonio at an outdoor table at a very busy, noisy restaurant. They asked us to join them, and after ordering pizza and mineral water, I broached the subject of my parents.

Zeca said he refused to let his concern about seeing my parents again block Antonio from seeing Crisanto playing one of the last games of the season.

That encouraged me, and a few days later, we were all in Genoa for the big match.

My parents loved Crisanto, and I couldn't believe how well we all got along. My dad and Antonio really hit it off. My mother fussed over Zeca, and it seemed all the old wounds had healed. I couldn't have been happier. After a wonderful dinner at our favorite pizza place, my father and Antonio awoke the next morning full of fire over insulting remarks made about Genoa on a local TV station's pre-game coverage.

"We'll show them who's boss!" my father warned. He and Antonio embarrassed me, my mom, and Zeca at the very explosive match against Milan.

"They must never be allowed out to a soccer game together again," my mother said with a stoic air, hiding behind a gigantic pair of Chanel sunglasses.

My father had to be cautioned by local officials. Twice. He was proud of that.

I thought Crisanto would be really pissed, but he said, "Your father was absolutely right. The umpire was a lunatic. A blind lunatic. I appreciated the family's support!"

As soon as we returned to the apartment, my mother cooked dinner, even though I tried to stop her. Crisanto raved about what I'd always thought of as British Boarding

School fare. "I've never eaten boiled chicken in my life," he said.

Zeca and I looked at each other and laughed.

"We should all go to Brazil to see *my* family," my lover announced.

"What do I wear?" my mum, ever the fashionista responded.

This began a discussion of weather, different times, and . . . the palace we were contemplating buying. My parents wanted to see it.

Crisanto called the contessa, and we grabbed a bottle of champagne and walked to her home. Of course, my parents were impressed . . . until my mother wormed her way into the parts of the property not normally on view.

It was a catastrophe.

"My God," my father said. "She's a hoarder!"

I could hardly believe what the contessa had done to the exquisite, ancient palace. She'd removed doors, wall sconces, light fixtures and had inexplicably stacked cartons, newspapers . . . all manner of trash in each and every room. The higher we went in the building, the worse it got.

"We must rescue it," Crisanto told me. "We must save this queen of the Baroque dynasty."

In Italy, even a desperate woman will drag her feet, and although Crisanto and I began negotiations to purchase the property, it could, in all likelihood, take months to actually finalize it. In the meantime, I returned to my life as a waiter.

My parents returned to London, my mother already practicing the words, "My son, who owns a palace in Italy . . ."

As usual, it was hard saying goodbye to my man who now told me he loved me. Constantly.

Back in Capri, we began getting ready for Hugh and Alex's wedding in Madrid, now that the summer tourists had gone, and the days grew more comfortable and relaxed.

Crisanto had already said he would come with me to Madrid. The happy couple had even pushed forward their big day to accommodate Crisanto's very last game of the season.

It always felt so good to be with him. He was my obsession. I knew I was his because we whispered it often. In bed, or out of it, what he thought, ate, touched, worked with . . . it's all I cared about. He in turn always wanted photos, details . . . minutiae of my day.

I'd never known a man like him. And he, of course, reciprocated. It took me a while to realize he was me . . . except his discipline was physical. He focused on football the way I'd focused on acting.

"There's something we need to discuss," he said to me one evening by phone as we talked what he'd need to pack to come visit me the next day.

"Should I be worried?" I asked as I demolished a sizzling platter of fried squid at Al Buco. I'd promised not to have our favorite pizza there until he was with me the following day.

"No, I hope not. But I want to ask you in person. I love you, Marius."

"I love you, too."

Neither of us slept much that night. We talked until late and fell asleep Skyping. Our signal vanishing was the only reason we stopped. My eyes drifted shut with my laptop in my arms. I jolted awake a few hours later, and I went outside.

It was dawn, and the sky was the colors of his rossoblu jersey.

I stood on the steps across from the front of the house, hoping beyond hope that his ferry was already crossing the harbor. It was ridiculous, I knew. But love had bitten me. It had bitten me badly.

And as I turned and walked back to the house, I heard a

soft barking sound. I was astonished to see Toppy creeping out of Angie's house in his underwear. Big man panties with a small dog in his arms. He set him to the ground, and the dog ran straight to the spot where I'd recently stood. The small, white, fluffy thing crouched and dropped a big load. I'd never seen such a big mound from such a tiny creature.

"Good boy, Brutus," Toppy said. He never even noticed me as he picked up the dog and took him back inside.

Holy mother of . . . Toppy was our dog scofflaw!

Antonio didn't believe me when I called at a more reasonable hour to tell him. He rushed up to the house and saw the mound of doo-doo and looked at me.

"You say he has a dog? But neither he or Angie ever registered a dog."

He pounded on their door. Angie opened it, hollering about the fragile state of her bread.

"Where's the dog?" he asked.

"What dog?" She tried pumping up her boobies, but Antonio was immune to her charms. He followed her inside. I could hear a lot of yelling, some tears, and some barking.

Antonio emerged looking upset.

"How is it going to appear . . . that I am the detective on this island, and they had a dog . . . that they hid . . . right under my nose?"

He scooped up a sample, not that it would help. He knew who the culprit was, and he was worried.

"I didn't mean to upset you so much, Antonio . . ." I began.

He let out a heavy sigh. "Ah well . . . it was bound to come out sooner or later. I can probably kiss my promotion goodbye." He stomped down the infernal stairs, and I felt like a heel. An utter, total heel.

I called Crisanto, who was boarding his plane.

"Don't blame yourself," he said. "And he's right. It was bound to come out sooner or later. It's over now."

But it wasn't. News had spread, and Toppy became the object of ridicule. People laughed and joked, so he stayed away from his own café. With none of us showing the slightest hint of gossiping with the customers, the furor died down by midafternoon. I kept eyeing the lemon wall-clock, counting the minutes until I knew Crisanto was on the inter-island ferry.

I dashed out of Toppy's, pacing the promenade until Crisanto arrived on the funicular. It was the hardest thing ever to greet him in public and not be able to touch him. We debated which was closer, the café or the house. We decided it was the café and ran to it.

We barricaded ourselves in the pantry, and he pushed me up against the shelves.

"You're gonna get fucked, Marius, if you answer the question right."

"Ask me."

"Will you move to Genoa to be with me?"

"Fuck, yes. Watch how fast I pack."

"Not yet. I want you first then I want some pizza."

He devoured my mouth with his, his gorgeous hands holding my ass to him. My cock grazed against his—and then the screaming started.

"What the—" His eyes widened, and we stopped what we were doing.

We ran outside and found the café in chaos.

"What's going on?" I asked.

"The mayor found out Dad's dog is the one that's been leaving poop everywhere. He's gonna wreck our business!" Zeca said.

Outside the café, I was astounded to see a huge crowd forming.

"My Yelp rating!" Toppy, who'd showed up finally, looked on the verge of tears. "They're gonna treat me like a criminal!"

He peered outside. "They don't have gallows from way back anywhere on the island, do they?"

I stood by helplessly as the mayor hosted his impromptu press conference with a subdued Antonio standing beside him. He looked dejected and miserable as the mayor said, "I can now reveal to you the owner of the dog that—"

"Wait!" said a voice.

I looked to my right. "Crisanto . . . what are you doing?"

"Do you love me?" he asked. "I mean . . . really love me?"

"Of course I love you."

He grabbed my hand. Everyone had stopped and stared. I could see the mayor didn't like his thunder being ripped from under his designer shoes.

"Wait!" Crisanto said again, ripping the mic out of the man's hand. It was almost like watching Kanye West doing his little number on Taylor Swift.

"I have an announcement to make!" Crisanto stared at the crowd. He looked confident, happy.

"We discovered the owner of the dog is an old resident who . . . well . . . let's just say didn't think that she was breaking any rules, but she'll be paying her fines. I'd also like to add that my name is Crisanto Alvarenga. I play soccer—some of you may call it football. I play for Genoa." Deep breath.

I stared at him. Oh . . . no . . . he wasn't—

"And I am gay."

The crowd went crazy. I was surprised how many people cheered, and I realized half of them were my own family members.

"I'm coming out because I love this man—" He held my hand up higher. "We love each other. And I won't live in secret. I can't hide how I feel because he is my relentless obsession. I'm gay, and I am proud of it."

The crowd loved it. The mayor was kissing our cheeks, people started pouring limoncellos for the cameras and Crisanto's mouth was all over mine.

He posed for photos. He seemed so happy.

Antonio hugged us both.

Toppy was crying.

"You threw yourself under the bus for me?" he kept asking Crisanto.

"We're family," Crisanto said. "That's what families do."

The two silver foxes came to join us, hugging us and congratulating Crisanto.

"You've taken a giant step for European athletes," they told him. "We are with you all the way."

The press conference dissolved with a lot of well-wishing . . . but as far as I was concerned, obsession worked both ways. I took my honey back to the pantry, even though he'd just jumped out of the closet.

"Now," I said, jamming it firmly shut with a few pallets of mineral water.

"Where were we?"

"Let me show you," he said.

And began to do so.

Relentlessly . . .

YOU MAY ALSO ENJOY THE FOLLOWING FROM EXTASY BOOKS INC:

Relentless Love
A.J. Llewellyn

Excerpt

Damn. I couldn't believe it. I hurried home, wondering what I would say if I called Hugh . . . or even if I should call. I started climbing the stairs to our house and stopped. No time like the present. I got Hugh's voicemail. I left a message, letting him know we'd be there tomorrow.

Back home, the house was empty. I thought Toppy must have been next door at Angelina's, or he wasn't home yet. I threw some clothes and a couple of books into a small suitcase and packed my laptop in its computer bag. Then I lay on my bed, my mind racing. Hugh was more attached to his cell phone than I was. It was weird he hadn't called back. I got out of bed, restless. I went downstairs then called a second and a third time, and even a fourth. I left two voicemail messages and a text.

Holy moly, he was ignoring me. What if he didn't want to see me? Then I'd be stuck!

I could hear impassioned sounds coming from Angelina's. I rolled my eyes. Dad was getting, er . . . lucky. Unbelievable. In spite of all the creepy things she'd been doing, he couldn't help himself. He still had to get his love. I sure wished I could call my brother, but I knew he was probably busy getting lucky, too.

Two seconds later, my cell phone rang. It was Zeca.

"What's wrong?" he asked. "I can feel you. Why didn't you call me?"

"Hugh isn't returning my calls."

"Where are you?"

"I'm home."

A long pause. "Give him a chance, Alex. He'll call you."

"No, he won't, and I'm gonna look like an ass showing up in St. Tropez tomorrow."

Another pause. I could hear him talking to Antonio.

"We're on our way."

I took a big breath and waited. I thanked whatever lucky stars I had that my brother had tuned into me and called. I found myself being more upset than I had been in a long time. For the first time in two weeks, I allowed myself to think back to the night Hugh, and I had fought, and he'd left the island.

We'd had a wonderful start to our evening. It had been my evening off. We spent the whole afternoon in bed. I swallowed over the lump forming in my throat. I'd taken for granted that he was staying with me. We got along so well. Our sex life was giddy, our kisses endless. I had never met a man who enjoyed kissing as much as I did.

He surprised me with dinner at Da Paolino, a wonderful, romantic restaurant in the middle of a lemon grove, and . . . and . . .

He asked me to marry him.

ABOUT THE AUTHOR

A.J. Llewellyn is the author of almost three hundred published gay romance novels. A.J. lives in California, but dreams of living in Hawaii. Frequent trips to all the islands, bags of Kona coffee in the fridge and a healthy collection of Hawaiian records keep A.J. refueled.

A.J's passion for the islands led to writing a play about the last ruling monarch of Hawaii, Queen Lili'uokalani. A.J. has written a non-erotic novel about the overthrow of her kingdom written in diary form from her maid's point of view.

A.J. never lacks inspiration for male/male erotic romances and has to prise fingers from the computer keyboard to pursue other passions: collecting books on Hawaiiana, surfing and spending time with family, friends and animal companions.

A.J. Llewellyn believes that love is a song best sung out loud.

Webpage: www.ajllewellyn.com
Facebook: www.facebook.com/aj.llewellyn
Twitter: www.twitter.com/ajllewellyn
Email: ajllewellyn@gmail.com